United States Congress

Memorial Addresses on the Life and Character of Charles Frederick Crisp

late a Representative from Georgia - delivered in the House of Representatives and

Senate, Fifty-fourth Congress, second session

United States Congress

Memorial Addresses on the Life and Character of Charles Frederick Crisp
late a Representative from Georgia - delivered in the House of Representatives and Senate,
Fifty-fourth Congress, second session

ISBN/EAN: 9783337378219

Printed in Europe, USA, Canada, Australia, Japan

Cover: Foto ©Andreas Hilbeck / pixelio.de

More available books at **www.hansebooks.com**

54TH CONGRESS, } HOUSE OF REPRESENTATIVES. { DOCUMENT
2d Session. } { No. 255.

MEMORIAL ADDRESSES

ON THE

LIFE AND CHARACTER

OF

CHARLES FREDERICK CRISP

(LATE A REPRESENTATIVE FROM GEORGIA),

DELIVERED IN THE

HOUSE OF REPRESENTATIVES AND SENATE,

FIFTY-FOURTH CONGRESS, SECOND SESSION.

PUBLISHED BY ORDER OF CONGRESS.

WASHINGTON:
GOVERNMENT PRINTING OFFICE.
1897.

CONTENTS.

. . . . —

3

PROCEEDINGS IN THE HOUSE—Continued.

PROCEEDINGS IN THE SENATE 161

Death of Charles Frederick Crisp.

Proceedings in the House.

December 7, 1896.

Mr. Turner, of Georgia. Mr. Speaker, it is my painful duty to have to announce to the House the untimely death of my colleague Charles Frederick Crisp, late a member of this body, which occurred in the city of Atlanta, Ga., on the 23d day of October last.

At some later day in the session I will ask the House to appoint a time when his friends here may pay fitting tribute to his distinguished character and to his eminent public services. At the present time I offer the following resolutions for immediate consideration.

The Clerk read as follows:

Resolved, That the House has heard with profound sorrow of the death of Hon. Charles Frederick Crisp, late a Representative from the State of Georgia.

Resolved, That as a mark of respect to his memory the House do now adjourn.

Resolved, That the Clerk communicate these resolutions to the Senate.

The resolutions were agreed to; and accordingly the House (at 3 o'clock and 45 minutes p. m.) adjourned until 12 o'clock to-morrow (Tuesday).

5

The SPEAKER. The Clerk will report the special order.

The Clerk read as follows:

Resolved, That Saturday, January 16, 1897, beginning at 1 o'clock p. m., be set apart for paying a tribute to the memory of the Hon. CHARLES F. CRISP, late a member of the House of Representatives from the State of Georgia.

Mr. TURNER, of Georgia. Mr. Speaker, I offer the resolutions which I send to the Clerk's desk.

The SPEAKER. The gentleman from Georgia [Mr. Turner] offers the following resolutions, which will be reported by the Clerk of the House.

The Clerk read as follows:

Resolved, That the business of the House be now suspended, that opportunity may be given for tributes to the memory of Hon. CHARLES F. CRISP, late a Representative from the State of Georgia.

Resolved, That as a mark of respect to the memory of the deceased, and in recognition of his eminent abilities as a distinguished public servant, the House, at the conclusion of these memorial proceedings, shall stand adjourned.

Resolved, That the Clerk communicate these resolutions to the Senate.

Resolved, That the Clerk be instructed to communicate a copy of these resolutions to the family of the deceased.

7

ADDRESS OF MR. TURNER.

Mr. TURNER. Mr. Speaker, CHARLES FREDERICK CRISP was born on the 29th of January, 1845. In the month of May, 1861, while he was still but a lad, he enlisted in the Army of the Confederate States, and his service was thenceforth rendered in the State of Virginia. At the end of the war, when he had still not reached his majority, he studied law, and was admitted to the bar in 1866. Soon thereafter he became solicitor-general of his judicial circuit, was reappointed to that honorable station, and then became judge of the superior court, in which high station he served for five years, and was then nominated for Congress.

Appearing on this floor during the Forty-eighth Congress, he was reelected consecutively six times. He became Speaker of the House of Representatives during two terms, and during the present Congress, by the nomination of his party associates, he became leader of his party.

During a prior Congress, and while he was Speaker, the governor of Georgia tendered him an ad interim appointment to the Senate of the United States, to fill the vacancy caused by the death of the late Gen. Alfred H. Colquitt. That honorable position he declined. During the present Congress he became a candidate for a regular term in the Senate, to begin on the 4th day of March next, and in the early part of October last a general assembly was chosen in Georgia, which would in a few weeks, with practical unanimity, have elected him to the Senate. He died on the 23d day of October last, a few weeks after his last great success.

The remarkable eminence which he attained seems greater when contrasted with his humble beginning. His training in the schools was limited. While yet a youth he joined the Confederate Army, and had not reached his majority when the war ceased. From a military prison he went forth to the struggle of life, without education and without resources, amid a people prostrated by a great defeat in war and impoverished by its desolating consequences. He was the foster child of adversity. In the camp, on the march, and in battle he learned lessons more difficult than those taught in the schools. There is not in all the varied round of human experience a more pathetic trial than that of a tender youth suddenly subjected to the horrors of war. But the lad who can bear strain and endure privation and face danger and death may in peace climb the dizzy heights to an elevation next to the highest in the world. His great career ended in his prime. His bright day closed at its noontide. He left this last field of honor without the sting of defeat and amid the cheers of victory. But, sir, between my late colleague and myself there was a wide difference of opinion. I leave to others the pleasant task of delineating the traits of character which endeared him to his friends, and of recounting the steps by which he rose to the highest places of power and responsibility.

ADDRESS OF MR. HENDERSON.

Mr. HENDERSON. Mr. Speaker, a sad duty engages our attention to-day. We are here to review the life, services, and character of our distinguished colleague and ex-Speaker of this House, CHARLES FREDERICK CRISP.

To his own delegation will be assigned the sacred duty of pointing out historically the leading actions of his life. I will briefly consider Mr. CRISP from the standpoint of my personal acquaintance and relationship with him as a member of this body.

This House presents in a marked degree evidence of the great law of change affecting all the relations of life. Mr. CRISP commenced his service as a member of this body in the Forty-eighth Congress. When he died there were only twelve members in the Fifty-fourth Congress who had served continuously with him from the time he entered Congress, and twenty in the same Congress who served with him in the Forty-eighth. He was one of seven elected to the Fifty-fourth Congress who were removed by death. These facts suggest the uncertainty of all life's positions and of life itself.

My relations with Mr. CRISP have been somewhat singular. He was the first member of Congress with whom I held heated debate, and I believe I was the last with whom he had debate developing some of the feelings so often incident to our legislative life, but leaving no scar. Our relations always, saving our first experience, were of the most friendly character, and our first sharp encounter taught us, I believe, to respect each other.

Though never intimate with Mr. CRISP in that sense

which means comradeship, so necessary to my life, we were always good friends, enjoying thoroughly cordial relations and mutual respect. I soon learned that his word once given to me was sacredly kept.

He was a man of high honor, and self-respect was a dominating element in his character.

He was truly a strong, deep, and earnest character. He was never a trifler.

He was kind and gentle in his manner, so much so in ordinary relations that one often wondered at the high and intense feeling which at times he was capable of swiftly reaching.

Some are constituted so as to move through life on a dead, cold level; others sound all the notes of life, reveling in its sunlight, suffering in its shadows. The greatest lives know both storm and rest. The Pacific Ocean can woo to its waters, but can drive in terror to its shores.

These thoughts come from a study of Mr. CRISP in my fourteen years' relationship with him on this floor. He had in his nature the sunlight and the shadow, the tempest and the calm.

Entering the Confederate Army as a mere boy of about 16, he soon learned how very serious a matter life was. It tempered the good metal until it was capable of great work, and the boy without a boyhood was soon a powerful and aggressive man. His strength and ability invited the confidence of the people, who soon elevated him, step after step, until, in this body, he reached a position of power second only to that of the Chief Executive.

When death took him, he had not yet attained the fullest stature of his mind.

The great Georgian sleeps—after a hard, active, tireless summer's work and before the autumn's harvest had come.

ADDRESS OF MR CATCHINGS.

Mr. CATCHINGS. Mr. Speaker, it has long been a custom with the House of Representatives, upon the death of one of its members, to set apart a day upon which addresses may be delivered for the purpose of placing upon its records in suitable form evidence of the esteem in which he was held. It is exceedingly difficult to prepare remarks for such purpose which shall be in all particulars appropriate. We are prone to indulge in fulsome eulogy, or, in the effort to avoid that, to fall short of paying just tribute. On this occasion, to me the task is peculiarly trying. The relations between CHARLES FREDERICK CRISP and myself were so intimate, my affection for him was so great, and my estimate of his character and abilities so high, that I shrink from speaking of him as they would naturally prompt me to do. The strong qualities which enabled him to grasp and retain the unchallenged leadership of his party in the House of Representatives, and which twice gave him its Speakership, manifested themselves in his boyhood, and steadily grew in potency and brilliancy up to the very hour of his death. He entered the Confederate Army when a slender lad but 16 years of age. Notwithstanding his extreme youth, he was soon elected to a lieutenancy of his company. Had he not been made a prisoner of war in May, 1864, and confined as such until hostilities had ended, there can be little doubt that he would have earned and achieved still higher and more responsible rank. Within five years from his admission to the bar he was appointed solicitor-general for one of the judicial circuits of his State, and in 1873 was reappointed for a term of four years.

His advancement in his profession was so rapid that in 1877 he was appointed judge of the superior court of the same circuit, and he was afterwards twice elected to that office. In 1882 he was elected a Representative in Congress, and was six times successively reelected. Almost from the day of his entrance into the House of Representatives he was recognized as one of its foremost members. In the Forty-ninth Congress, as a member of the Committee on Commerce, in the absence of its distinguished chairman, he had in charge the bill to create the Interstate Commerce Commission and define its jurisdiction and powers. That measure elicited prolonged, earnest, and serious debate, and the great skill and ability displayed by him in defending it and securing its passage gave him rank among the strongest and most useful Representatives. He had already, in the Forty-eighth Congress, given evidence of that remarkable grasp and perception of parliamentary law which was speedily to develop until he became one of its acknowledged masters. It will be remembered that the seat of Hon. John G. Carlisle, the Speaker of the Fiftieth Congress, was contested. This made it improper that the members of the Committee on Elections, which would be charged with the duty of examining into and reporting upon this contest, should be appointed by him. It was therefore provided that the committee should be chosen directly by the House of Representatives.

Hon. Henry G. Turner, of Georgia, then as now an honored Representative, had been chairman of that committee in the Forty-ninth Congress, and in that capacity had rendered most useful and distinguished service. He declined to serve longer on that committee. Mr. CRISP'S power in debate, professional acquirements, and aptitude for parliamentary management had been so notable that, as by one impulse, his Democratic colleagues, though against his will, selected him for the chairmanship of that committee. His work in connection with it was of such high order that when the Fiftieth Congress ended, he had greatly advanced himself in public estimation as well as in the regard of his colleagues. In the Fifty-first Congress, which had passed under Republican control, he was the senior member of the Democratic minority of the Committee on Elections. Though not holding a committee assignment of such character as according to the precedents invested him with the highest rank, yet, immediately upon Mr. Carlisle's retirement from this body to occupy the seat in the Senate to which he had been elected, by sheer force of his remarkable fitness he immediately forged to the front and seized the actual, substantial leadership of his party, which was never wrested from him until he had closed his eyes in his last and eternal sleep. No good purpose can be subserved by recalling the fierce and frequent struggles which marked the stormy career of that Congress.

It is sufficient to say that this gallant and courageous leader was ever in the thick of the fight, battling bravely for the right as he saw it, and that amid all the heat and fury of the turbulent scenes then enacted his mind was ever clear, his aims definite, his purpose unfaltering, and his poise of character so magnificent and superb as to challenge the respect and admiration of the whole country. When it became known that the Fifty-second Congress would have a Democratic majority, he was at once a candidate for the Speakership. His candidacy was not of his own making. It came about upon the insistence of a large number of his party colleagues, who, witnessing his steady growth, the wonderful versatility he had displayed in the discharge of every duty to which he had been assigned, and above all the masterful qualities which had distinguished his conduct amid the trying events of the Fifty-first Congress, desired that he should be elevated to the Speakership and charged with the grave responsibilities pertaining to that exalted office. The contest over the Speakership of the Fifty-second Congress was one of the most memorable in the annals of the House of Representatives. With no external influences to aid him, victory came to him through the sheer force of his strong and attractive personality and the profound admiration excited by the eminent services he had rendered his party under circumstances which displayed to advantage his great and forceful qualities. During this contest bitter attacks were made upon him from many sources, but his character was so lofty and his qualifications so conspicuous that the shafts of misrepresentation and calumny fell harmless at his feet. He did not regard his election as in any sense a personal triumph, and I know that he entered upon the duties of the office of Speaker with as pure and patriotic emotions as ever animated the human breast.

The difficulties and responsibilities attendant upon that office are known to few outside of this Chamber, and in all their details they are not fully appreciated by many of us here. The Speaker appoints all the committees of the House. This power of appointment, conferred upon him by our rules, enables him in a large measure to give color to all important legislation which may be proposed by the several committees. The pressure upon him by members of the House for such assignments as their ambition or tastes may lead them to desire is persistent and tremendous.

While he can not and should not turn an indifferent ear to the claims of his friends and supporters, yet he must not forget that the responsibility for legislation rests largely upon him, and that beyond certain limitations, if he would have the best work done, he can not afford to be influenced by personal considerations or the inclinations of friendship. And in any event, even where all considerations are equal, his appointments can not be shaped so as to satisfy the expectations or desires of all.

Under the rules of the House, very few of the committees have the privilege of calling up for consideration at any time bills reported by them. Committees not possessing this privilege, and members interested in bills reported by them, are constantly importuning the Speaker to allow such measures to be acted upon. This imposes upon him the burden of examining these bills, passing judgment upon them, and determining whether or not he will intervene to secure their consideration by the House. In the very nature of things he feels the necessity in the large majority of instances of this sort to refuse his intervention. While the Speaker is not so separated from the membership of the House as that, as in the case of the Speaker of the British House of Commons, he must cease to be a partisan when he assumes the duties of his office, yet as to all questions not involved in party policy it is incumbent upon him to deal fairly and impartially with all the members of the House. A man so constituted that he can not as to such nonpartisan questions be absolutely just and equitable is not qualified for the office of Speaker. No man can satisfactorily discharge the functions of the Speakership who is not a good judge of human nature. He must understand that there are "many men of many minds;" that peculiarities of temperament exist among the members of this House as elsewhere; that some of them are insistent and persistent, while others are diffident and shrinking; that some are extremely sensitive and easily wounded, while others are phlegmatic and not of so fine a mold; that self-assertiveness and loquacity are not always, or even usually, accompanied by the best ability, and finally that, generally stated, each member is fairly striving to serve his constituency according to the lights before him.

How well Mr. CRISP met the requirements of the Speaker's office there are many here and elsewhere who can attest. His kindly and patient consideration of all requests made of him was notorious. He was always accessible, and neither by word nor manner gave offense to those whose official duties compelled them to approach him. Amid all the pressure upon him, even after his health was broken and the burdens of the office seemed more than he could bear, as Clarendon said of the great Hampden, "He preserved his own natural cheerfulness and vivacity, and above all a flowing courtesy to all men." Indeed, his nature was so kindly and his desire to possess the esteem and friendship of his colleagues so intense, that even when it must have cost him great effort he would assume that cordial manner and cheery smile so familiar to all of us in this Chamber. In dispensing the privileges at his disposal regarding the proceedings of the House he was absolutely impartial, and neither friend nor foe ever suspected that he had not received from him fair and equitable treatment.

As a presiding officer he has had few equals. His presence in the Speaker's chair was so fine and manly, his voice so full and resonant, and his alertness and power in dealing with parliamentary problems so manifest, that it was always a pleasure to onlookers to witness the superb manner in which he presided over our deliberations. Misunderstandings and collisions between members sometimes occur to mar the proceedings here, and of these he had his share, as was to be expected in view of his strong character and prominent position. But he never sought to provoke these troubles, and I have many times heard him express the keenest regret that he had been drawn into them. He was a very ambitious man, but his ambition was to render honorable service to his country, and not to exalt himself. He believed in the teachings, principles, and traditions of the Democratic party, and therefore was an earnest partisan. But his partisanship was not of that cheap quality which eternally proclaims itself lest it be overlooked, nor was it ever displayed in such manner as to be personally offensive to others. While his opinion was firm upon all subjects that he had investigated, he was more. than scrupulous in yielding respect to the judgment of those who differed with him. He recognized the right of all men to think for themselves, and imputed no improper motives or lack of ability to those who had reached conclusions and expressed opinions different from his own.

This fairness upon his part was ever displayed in his official capacity as Speaker as well as in private intercourse. During the extra session of 1893, when the House of Representatives was called upon to deal with the important financial question then presented for its consideration, although he was an earnest advocate of the free coinage of silver, his official conduct was so fair and exempt from all personal bias or prejudice that no man, whatever his views may have been, could have pointed to any word or act of his upon which to base complaint or criticism. And as in this instance, so it ever was with him in dealing with great public questions. I do not hesitate to affirm that throughout his Congressional career, from its beginning to the end, he displayed the highest qualities of leadership, and that he was ever guided by aspirations and sentiments altogether ennobling. The distinguished Speaker of this House, in a telegram of condolence sent upon his death to his bereaved widow, truly said that his loss is the country's. He had rendered his country great and valuable service, and, being yet in the prime of life, he had abundant resources upon which, if life had been spared, he would freely and proudly have drawn in its interest and behalf.

His services as Speaker of the Fifty-second Congress were so notable and satisfactory to his party that he was reelected to the Speakership of the Fifty-third Congress without opposition, and in the Fifty-fourth Congress, which had passed under Republican control, he was complimented by the unanimous vote of his party associates for that office. During the Fifty-third Congress he was tendered by the governor of Georgia the appointment as Senator to fill the vacancy created by the death of Senator Colquitt. It was no small part of his ambition to represent his State in that august body. Accompanying this tender came telegrams from distinguished citizens of Georgia who aspired to the vacant seat in the Senate, pledging him that if he would accept the appointment he should have no opposition for election before the legislature. He did not feel that under the existing circumstances he would be justified in vacating the Speakership, and therefore promptly put aside the tempting object of his ambition. In talking with him on the subject I suggested that the opportunity to attain a seat in the Senate might never come to him again, and insisted that he was not called upon to perform such an act of self-abnegation. Other friends tendered him similar advice. He could not view the situation in that light, and so, placing country and party above self, he declined the great honor, and so far as outward appearances indicated without the slightest pain or even regret. And yet I knew, as many of his friends did, that he desired almost above all things to be a Senator from the State of Georgia. No finer act was ever performed by a public man, and it is in itself ample proof of the nobility of his soul and the loftiness of his character. The people of his State, remembering his unselfish sacrifice, upon the announcement by Senator Gordon in the spring of last year that he would not seek reelection, promptly determined that Mr. CRISP should be his successor, and although considerable effort was made to organize opposition, yet the admiration and respect of the people for him was so unbounded that it was swept away like chaff before the wind; and at the general primaries held throughout the State in the summer and fall of 1896 he was chosen as the Democratic nominee by a substantially unanimous vote. But the legislature of Georgia was not permitted to ratify this verdict of the people by investing him with formal title to a seat in the United States Senate.

The disorder from which he had long been suffering suddenly struck him down on the 23d day of October, 1896, and, as with Moses of old, when in sight of the goal of his ambition, his noble spirit took its flight from all earthly scenes. The deep and widespread regret which at once, through telegrams, letters, resolutions, and otherwise, manifested itself in all sections of the country gave evidence of the profound impression created throughout the United States by his eminent public services and of the high and affectionate esteem in which he was almost universally held. In the State of Georgia, upon which his splendid career had reflected such honor, the grief of the people knew no bounds, and was manifested by many and impressive public ceremonials. For a time his body lay in state in the capitol at Atlanta, where multitudes of both sexes and of all ages and colors thronged to view it. It was then carried to his home in Americus upon a special train, escorted by the whole body of State officials and a delegation of judges in behalf of the judiciary of the State. At all the stations along the route vast crowds gathered, in many instances accompanied by military organizations, and often insisting upon having the casket opened that they might once more behold the features of their honored dead. In Americus, his home, where he was revered by his neighbors for his great achievements and loved for his affectionate and generous nature, upon every building, whether private or public, emblems of mourning were profusely displayed. Large delegations from every community in his Congressional district gathered there to participate in the funeral rites. On the 25th day of October, amid the tears and lamentations of that vast assemblage, our honored friend and distinguished colleague was tenderly laid away in his last resting place.

I have not yet spoken of his domestic relations; indeed, I scarce know how to speak of them. They may be summed up in the statement that he was a devoted husband and a loving father. I doubt if in his family circle a harsh word or rude sentiment ever escaped his lips. When with his wife and children, his sweetness of temper, gentle care, and kindly consideration were beyond all power of description.

The character of our distinguished friend easily accounts for the true and real leadership acquired and so long retained by him in the House of Representatives and elsewhere. I say elsewhere, for, as I have already pointed out, he was under all conditions and circumstances a true and real leader. He was wholly exempt from every species of charlatanry. He had no trick of voice or deportment to distinguish him from others. He never strutted or posed or affected an air of wisdom or assumed a patronizing manner. In social life he never discoursed, but contented himself with conversation, and that was always frank and polite, and especially marked by kindly consideration for others. He did not need to be bolstered up by such cheap and tawdry devices. For affectations of all sorts indeed he had great contempt, often saying that they are the sure concomitants of weakness and vulgarity. His official conduct was ever courteous and dignified. Though possessing great faculty for retort in debate, and making use of it whenever it seemed to be the most effective weapon, yet it was of the kind that, though smarting at the time, left no permanent sting behind. His sagacity was such that he rarely took a false step in the management of the cause he had in hand. His success is largely attributable to the fact that he lost sight of himself entirely while discharging his official duties. I doubt if he was ever suspected of performing for the sake of self-aggrandizement. His integrity of purpose, so far as I know, was never questioned, and I am sure that it could never have been successfully impeached. The traits I have described, coupled with industry, unceasing vigilance, exceptional power in debate, and a mental

poise which nothing could disturb, commanded the admiration, respect, and confidence of his party colleagues, and
caused them instinctively to turn to him for advice and
counsel.   They knew that he faithfully endeavored to serve
his country and party; that no desire for personal preferment ever marred his purpose or directed his conduct; that
he was alert and sagacious, studious and thoughtful, careful and prudent.   Such a man could not fail to be a leader,
no matter what might be his environments.   My personal
devotion to him was great, and I had abundant cause to
know that it was fully and cordially reciprocated.   It gives
me infinite pleasure to reflect that the friendship between
us was never impaired, and that to the very last I was the
recipient of his love and confidence.   With me no other
can take his place.

ADDRESS OF MR. DALZELL.

Mr. DALZELL. Mr. Speaker, it seems difficult of belief that, while we are engaged from day to day in the routine of Congressional life and strife, one who but lately was in the forefront of every battle on this floor is sleeping his last sleep in the soil of his Georgian home. It requires our positive knowledge of a melancholy fact to persuade us that a glance across the aisle will not disclose his presence in his accustomed seat. His cheery voice, his kindly look, the warm grasp of his hand, I can hardly realize that they may not be with me on the morrow. But they will not. He who was the leader of his party here and a potential factor when the first session of this Congress ended, ere its second session began, at the call of Providence, joined the great majority who have "passed over the river and are resting under the shade of the trees."

The thoughts suggested by an occasion like this, while they are of the most solemn, interesting, and suggestive character, are nevertheless trite and commonplace in their expression. True, they bring us face to face with the unsolved and insoluble problem of immortality. But death is the common destiny of all. Men have been dying since the world began; and with each death the same queries have been made and have failed of answer. There is no oracle outside of Revelation to make reply. What that country is, or whether any, to which we all are bound no man shall know save the emigrant thereto. From him no answer comes; and philosophy and speculation are vain. There is no retreat save to the faith so aptly defined by the great

apostle as "the substance of things hoped for, the evidence
of things not seen."

In bringing my humble but sincere tribute to the memory
of CHARLES FREDERICK CRISP, I shall not undertake to
recite at any length the history of his life. Others more
familiar with its details will do that, and they will do it
lovingly. The merest outline of it is sufficient to prove
him to have been a man of mark. Born to an inheritance
of struggle, without the advantages of wealth or influence
or great name, his native virtues, and these only, were the
factors in the problem of his successful fortune. His education was only that of the common schools—the common
schools that so many times have been the grand univer-
sities productive of the highest type of American citizenship. The greatest of modern English poets has idealized
such character in his conception of—

> Some divinely gifted man,
> Whose life in low estate began
> And on a simple village green;
>   Who breaks his birth's invidious bar,
> And grasps the skirts of happy chance,
> And breasts the blows of circumstance,
>   And grapples with his evil star;
> Who makes by force his merit known,
> And lives to clutch the golden keys,
> To mold a mighty state's decrees,
> And shape the whisper of the throne;
> And moving up from high to higher,
>   Becomes on Fortune's crowning slope
>   The pillar of a people's hope.

The language of eulogy, Mr. Speaker, is too apt to be
the language of extravagance, and the extravagant eulogist
overleaps his purpose. I would avoid that danger, and,
putting aside so much of the poet's language as would be
extravagant here, will simply say that the boy of nameless
birth, who by his own inherent strength became the Speaker

of the House of Representatives of the American people, has a right to be ranked as one who made by force his merit known, and lived to mold a mighty State's decrees.

Into the panorama of our friend's life there are woven many pictures. From a schoolboy he became a soldier; left home and kindred to follow the flag that stood to him for the right. That was not our flag. From our standpoint, he was mistaken; from his, he was a patriot. The time has long since gone by when dispute over that question may be had. And when he was borne, amid the lamentations of his people, to his last resting place, he could not have had (and I doubt not he himself would have said so) a more welcome shroud than the Stars and Stripes—the symbol of an indissoluble Union cemented in blood.

In civil life, with great distinction, he illustrated the versatility of American genius and the grand possibilities of American citizenship. It is characteristic of the American that he is a man of many sides. A possible ruler as well as one ruled—a factor in the creation and maintenance of enterprises which under our system of government depend upon individual effort instead of governmental—his education is that of experience, and is practical and varied. The life of our deceased friend proves the truth of this observation

He was a lawyer of mark—first, solicitor-general of his circuit; then clothed with the spotless ermine of a judge. It is said of him that in both of these capacities he measured up to the full stature of a perfect manhood. Retiring from his judgeship, he became the representative of his State on the floor of this House. Here there is no need to sound his praises. They are part and parcel of the plain records of the American Congress.

During his period of service many questions of national importance enlisted legislative attention. His attitude with respect thereto was the attitude of his party; and he was ever at the fore in the assertion and maintenance of that party's principles. All honor to him for that. All honor, say I always, to the man of strong and honest convictions who has the courage to stand by them.

In the assertion and maintenance of his chosen beliefs he was ever a leader. He possessed the elements of leadership. He was bold, aggressive, logical, convincing. He was inspiring; men loved to follow him. He was as brave in defeat as in victory. His leadership asserted itself; and by the choice of his party during two Congresses he presided with dignity in the great office of Speaker of this House.

I do not say that he was always right. I do not say that he had no faults. Far from it. He was a strong man and gentle; and his faults, such as they were, were overborne immensely by his virtues; and we have now no memory save for the latter.

And so now, with this simple tribute to his memory—so far short of its deserving—I leave him to his conspicuous place upon the roll of the nation's illustrious dead—among those whom the world delights and will continue to honor.

ADDRESS OF MR. RICHARDSON.

Mr. RICHARDSON. Mr. Speaker, on the first Monday of December, 1883, as a member of the Forty-eighth Congress, CHARLES FREDERICK CRISP took his seat in this House. I did not know him until the beginning of the Forty-ninth Congress, the first to which I was elected. Very early after the organization of the Forty-ninth Congress I was assigned to membership on the Committee on Pacific Railroads, of which he was also a member. In the arrangement of seats at the table of that committee I was placed by his side, and in this way first made his acquaintance. I was a new member, and although he had had then but one term, I found he was entirely familiar with all questions before the committee, and that its able and efficient chairman, Hon. J. W. Throckmorton, of Texas, and the entire committee trusted implicitly his opinions and his judgment.

The acquaintance thus formed between us grew into perfect friendship. There was never an incident of any kind or character from the date of our first meeting, through all the long years we served together in this House, that marred that friendship. It remained unbroken to his death. The reflection that throughout all his services here I had his esteem, his respect, and his friendship is a source of supreme satisfaction to me.

As a younger member of the House in service he always gave me his encouragement; as a coworker in committee he gave me his assistance; and finally, when he came to the highest position in the gift of this body, I rejoice to know I enjoyed his confidence and support. Each time when he sought the Speakership it was my pleasure to cast my vote for him; and on the occasion of his last nomination to that elevated station I had the honor (which I regarded a high one) by his request to formally present his name. On that occasion, among other things, I said:

The very pleasant task has been given me of placing in nomination for Speaker of the House in the Fifty-fourth Congress a gentleman who is my warm personal and political friend. It goes without saying that this gentleman has already been named for the position in the hearts of all of us here assembled, and it only remains for the formal words to be spoken. When the Fifty-second Congress was about to assemble, just four years ago now, there appeared in this Chamber 240 of the chosen representatives of a hopeful and triumphant Democracy. Then it was, after a sharp and brilliant contest, the gentleman I am to name was placed in the Speaker's chair. Two years later, when about 215 members of our party met here for a similar purpose, with the experience of a past Congress to guide us, with full knowledge of his honesty, capacity, and ability, he was by unanimous action and with hearty acclamation again chosen our leader. We come now a small band of patriots, so far as numbers are concerned, to say again he is our choice for this responsible office, but we recognize the fact that this time our declaration is impotent.

The roll was called, and he was unanimously chosen as our nominee.

It will not be expected of me on this occasion to enter into an account in detail of his long and useful career as a member of this House and a citizen of Georgia. This has been done to-day by others of this body by whom these things are said more appropriately than by myself. I shall content myself with speaking of him in a more general way.

The effort on my part to fully describe the loss the country, and more particularly the Democratic party, sustains by his untimely death would be a failure. There is no man in public life to-day who could not better be spared than Mr. CRISP. His place may be taken, but it can not be filled by any other Representative.

He enjoyed to the fullest capacity the confidence of his party not only on this floor, but throughout the Union. Those who differed with him here and elsewhere entertained for him marked respect. His powers in debate were of the very highest order, as all can testify who ever thus met him. He was always cool and clear-headed, and often quite aggressive. His courage was unsurpassed, as his supporters and opponents all will bear witness. His honesty was never questioned. His conduct was always above reproach. Called to the responsible and exacting duties of Speaker of the House, he met these responsibilities and duties in such manner as to reflect not only honor and credit upon himself and his party, but upon the entire country. In the chair he was always amiable, yet always positive. He was gentle, yet stern when duty demanded sternness in the Speaker. He loved to do deeds of kindness as a presiding officer, but never did them when it was improper to do them or when they were to be done at the expense of his office. He was gifted in the statement of all questions and was a talented parliamentarian. He was at all times composed, and while others grew excited, his self-possession was never for a moment disturbed. He was firm in his administration of the affairs of the House, and at times was quite emphatic, but he was always impartial, considerate, and just.

There are times, we all know, in this body when, amid the excitement incident to debate on exciting political questions, when party feeling is running high and bitterness of expression is freely indulged, to preserve order and fair decorum the occupant of that chair is called upon to exercise and must, in his discretion, exercise great powers. Yet during all his experience through many trying and exciting scenes he never exercised those powers rudely or too arbitrarily. He never on such occasions abused the prerogatives and powers of the Speaker or brought his high office into contempt.

I would not be understood as saying or insinuating that he was not a partisan, or, more strictly speaking, a party man. He was a strong believer in the principles and tenets of his party, and this with a man of his pronounced convictions and courage necessarily made him more or less a partisan; but his partisanship was never exerted at the expense of his patriotism. Though a partisan, he was not a fanatic.

His experience as a lawyer and judge made him conservative and fair-minded. He never for one moment permitted his partisanship to provoke in him bitterness of feeling or expression or to render him uncharitable toward his political opponents or those with whom he differed. He never impugned motives when engaged in controversies nor assailed character in partisan warfare.

His public record covers a period when courage, high ability, and absolute integrity were required to meet grave and important exigencies. It is a proud satisfaction to know that his connection with the history and his appearance in all these exigencies and emergencies were wholly honorable to himself and conspicuously serviceable to his State and country.

In unofficial life he was given the best opportunity to display those splendid traits of character which in him were so pronounced and distinguished. I have said he was honorable and just as a public man and presiding officer; so he was sincere and true as a private citizen. His was a changeless sincerity. He was never in disguise. He was the soul of honor. He had a contempt for everything low, mean, or sordid. Highly endowed as he was by nature and his own training with so many estimable traits, his influence over men was almost without limit.

He had no compromise to make with that which was wrong, and held with tenacity to that which he believed to be right.

He was warm-hearted, genial, and social in his nature. He enjoyed the companionship of friends, and made it both pleasant and agreeable for them to be with him. High toned, manly, and dignified in manner and conduct, he treated everyone, both high and low, in fashion becoming a gentleman, and expected like treatment in return.

He was in every respect a most lovable man.

All who came in close acquaintance or contact with him became his friends and admirers. He was a genuine type of the best element of the South. He was called before his work was finished. He did not die of old age or lingering delay. "His eye was not dim, nor his natural force abated."

He was an active worker until his life closed. The full measure of his capabilities had not been reached, and his career was incomplete. He was full of ambition, but was never sordid and venal. His ambitions were all noble.

One of his highest ambitions, as I have heard him say, was to represent Georgia in the United States Senate. Yet he was so self-sacrificing to his conception of the true sense of duty that, when the coveted seat was graciously tendered

him by the governor of his State, he declined it, saying his
first duty was not to himself, but to the House of Representatives, which had honored and trusted him.

He held the high office of judge before being elected to
Congress, and also filled other positions of responsibility
and dignity in his State.   In the late war between the
States he was a courageous soldier.   From his early manhood until death ended his bright and enviable career his
pathway had been strewn all along with honors, his hands
filled with trusts confided to him by his fellow-citizens,
his brain continuously occupied in anxious and arduous
thought, his body often taxed to the utmost of physical
endurance, but his course had been steadily and unfalter-
ingly upward.

When the end came, there was no stain upon his name
and fame.   He died in the maturity of his strength and in
the fullness of his powers.   The position he attained in his
country's pantheon is an elevated one.   His name will
survive long in the history of his State and the country.

A familiar writer has said, ''There is no antidote against
the opium of time,'' and that ''gravestones scarce tell the
truth forty years.''   It is vain for any man to hope for
immortality or for a patent from oblivion, for there is nothing really immortal but immortality.

It is a fact that only twenty-seven names of the multitude who lived make up the world's history before the
Flood.   The greater part of humanity by far must be content to be as though they had not been, and be found in
the register of God and not in the record of man.

I will not disparage the names of those who have gone
before him in the high office of Speaker of this House.
Many of them have been men of great renown and adorned

that exalted station, but none of them surpassed him in zeal and devotion to duty, none surpassed him in patriotism, honesty, and courage, and none exceeded him in energy and integrity. The best that can be said of any of them can be truthfully said of him.

His splendid and successful career was cut off when he was in his highest usefulness, and all must realize the irreparable loss his State and the Republic sustained when his incomplete life was terminated.

The story of his life illustrates what energy, honesty, integrity, and devotion to duty will achieve. That story will illumine the brightest page not only in Georgia's history, but that of our whole country; and his name, which passes as an invaluable heritage to his grief-stricken widow and children, will be preserved and perpetuated in spotless purity through a long hereafter.

ADDRESS OF MR. MADDOX.

Mr. MADDOX. Mr. Speaker, the distinguished gentlemen who have preceded me have in eloquent and beautiful language portrayed the life and character of my late distinguished colleague as a soldier, citizen, husband, father, lawyer, prosecuting officer, judge, member of Congress, and Speaker of this House, and but little is left for me to say. But there are some thoughts that I desire to suggest on this occasion. What has already been said of his merits, in my opinion, has not been exaggerated.

I first became acquainted with CHARLES FREDERICK CRISP in Atlanta in 1883, when he was presiding over a State convention for the purpose of nominating a governor, and met him occasionally until I became a member of the Fifty-third Congress, when my relations with him became exceedingly close, and I am proud to say that I enjoyed his confidence to a larger extent perhaps than any of his colleagues. He told me of his political troubles and trials. I knew his ambition to be a Senator from Georgia long before he made that fact known to the world, and when he was offered the appointment by Governor Northen, no one knew better than myself what it cost him to lay aside the goal of his ambition to discharge a patriotic duty that he owed the country; but he did it cheerfully.

When he determined to become a candidate for Senator, he departed from the usual custom that prevailed in our State in obtaining the voice of the people. Instead of going before the legislature, he demanded of the party machinery in the State that they order a primary election for United States Senator, and let every Democrat in Georgia speak for himself; and they did speak, and from the mountains to the seaboard, almost without a dissenting voice, he was chosen.   Through his long term of service in this House he was always the champion of the people and their rights, and when he aspired to a seat in the Senate, it was to the people he appealed and not to rings and combinations.   As high as he stood in the estimation of the people of his State, they never fully appreciated his great ability on the stump.   He never had any opposition that amounted to anything in his election in his own district, and, the State never being a doubtful one, therefore, when the great political contests were being fought throughout the Union, he was at the command of his party, and wherever the battle raged the warmest there he could be found at the front battling for Democracy.   So, when he went to Georgia to discuss the political issues of the day in joint debate with his distinguished fellow-citizen Hon. Hoke Smith and was compelled to discontinue them, some of the newspapers were unkind enough to attribute his withdrawal to an inability to cope with his distinguished and able adversary.

Mr. Speaker, we who have seen him cross swords with the ablest men in the House on every sort of question that it is possible to conceive of in a body like this, and found him to be the equal of any and inferior to none, and who knew of his great power and tact upon the stump before the people, were not prepared to believe this, and when he returned to his post here, I met him at his hotel and found him a sick man, and from what he said I knew that his disease was far more serious than mere throat trouble.   I sat beside him in the first session of the Fifty-fourth

Congress, and I know that after his return from Georgia he never arose to address the House but he complained of the great pain it gave him to do so. After Congress adjourned he went to Asheville, N. C., and spent the summer. There his friends hoped he would regain his health at that famous resort.

The reports we had from him from time to time led his friends to believe that he had been greatly benefited, and when he returned to Georgia in the early fall, I, at the instance of the citizens of Rome, invited him to address the people of that section on the political issues of the day. He accepted the invitation, and I met him at the depot the evening before he was to speak, and was astonished to see the inroads that disease had made upon him in the few months we had been separated. But, notwithstanding the fact that he was then at death's door, he bore up manfully and attended a reception that was held in his honor and had a hearty handshake and smile for all whom he met.

He was to speak the next morning at 11 o'clock. I called for him at 10 o'clock and was admitted to his room by his distinguished son, Charles R. Crisp, and found him upon the bed writhing in pain. After the paroxysms had to some extent passed off, I begged him not to attempt to make a speech. He said that he was advertised to speak; the people had come to hear him, and he was determined to make the effort. I accompanied him to the opera house and introduced him to the vast audience that had assembled there. He spoke for one hour and fifteen minutes, and, while he was not as vigorous as I had seen him when addressing the people before, he made one of the clearest, most logical, and powerful arguments that I ever heard from him. This speech was published throughout the

State and used as a campaign document. And yet, while he was speaking, I would not have been surprised to have seen him fall, and was expecting it; but with sheer force of will power, which he possessed in a wonderful degree, and with death staring him in the face, he coolly, deliberately, and courageously depicted the wrongs of the present financial system and told the people how they were to be corrected. This was his last speech, and it was worthy to be his last.

The people who heard him were delighted and were looking forward to the time when they could point to him as the Senator from Georgia. But alas! how little did they know of the condition of this man they were so eager to honor. Mr. Speaker, when he was leaving Rome, I begged him not to attempt to speak any more in the campaign. He finally agreed that he would not, though exceedingly anxious to visit several places in the State for that purpose. My opportunities for judging this man were good. I had his confidence. I sat by him. I watched him closely. I compared him with all the distinguished men that I knew or had ever known; and in my judgment, viewed from every phase of life, politically, socially, and otherwise, he was the peer of any and inferior to none.

When the death angel, with his solemn message, invaded our midst and summoned from earth this pure and spotless statesman, the nation mourned and every heart in Georgia was saddened, every eye was dimmed with tears; for they realized that a great and good man was gone and our country had sustained an irreparable loss—cut down in the strength and vigor of his manhood, when his ability and usefulness were recognized all over the country. Though he will mingle with us no more, and we will miss the

genial smile and the cordial hand clasp, though his voice
may be hushed and his chair may be vacant, yet the spirit
of patriotism and chivalry which he breathed into the
hearts of his countrymen will live for ages. We can not
dismiss him to the dark chambers of death. Recognizing
his greatness and goodness, we delight to do him honor,
and will weave bright garlands gathered from the sweetest
flowers of admiration, friendship, and love, and tenderly
twine them, a last sad tribute, around his memory.

ADDRESS OF MR. McMILLIN.

Mr. McMILLIN. Mr. Speaker, it is sad to have those at
any time of life go from us who are capable of serving their
country; but to have the gifted and patriotic taken in the
prime of life, when ability is at the zenith, when the enthu-
siasm of youth is happily blended with the discretion of
age, is the greatest loss the State can sustain in the death
of the citizen.

Such was the case in the death of CHARLES FREDERICK
CRISP. He had by hard work and superior intellectuality
fought the battles of early life and won. He had attained
an eminence in his State and country of which any man
might be justly proud. He had the respect and confidence
of his party and people in a very high degree. His State
stood ready to bestow upon him still greater honors. His
country was ready to applaud and ratify anything his State
did in his honor. A future full of brightness and distinction lay before him when the relentless reaper came and
claimed the harvest.

Mr. CRISP was one of the young men of the South who
came on the stage just in time to see his country rent asun-
der and distracted by a fierce fratricidal strife. Brave and
enthusiastic, he united his fortunes with those of his State
and section and risked his life in behalf of what he thought
was right. The close of the war found him still a youth,
in a land devastated by the ravages of war, with its agriculture prostrate, its educational institutions closed, many of
its young men buried on the battlefield, and sorrow and
waste hanging like a pall over the whole land. Such had

been the ruin around him that of the 11,000,000 people in the South the combined wealth of 7,000,000 would probably not have aggregated half a million dollars. Ruin stalked abroad where prosperity had only a few years before smiled on the whole land. There was everything to discourage, there was everything to dismay.

Such were the scenes which surrounded this young man on his return from the greatest war of modern times, and the greatest civil war of history. Like many other noble and strong young men of that day and land, Mr. CRISP saw these discouraging surroundings without dismay. Instead of giving up because his educational advantages had been restricted by these patriotic duties, he cast about him for the best means of restoring his country to its former prosperity and its prestige. He did not give up the struggle of life because the struggle at arms had been unsuccessful. He had confidence in the strength of his people, the resources of his land, and the power and permanency of free institutions.

Others who have preceded me have given so minute an account of his action at that period, the exertion he made, the success he attained, the trust reposed in him by an appreciating people, that it would be out of place for me to reiterate them; but it may be truly said that he was one of the hard-working and potent agencies in reviving the drooping spirits of the people around him and in building up the waste places of his loved land. Notwithstanding he died so young, he lived to see the agriculture of his country rise again. He lived to see the sails of commerce whiten the ocean and Gulf around him. He lived to see his own State one of the leaders in the manufacture of the cotton it produced. He lived to see the iron smelted in the valleys through which he had recently fought force its way by its superiority or cheapness to the markets not only of this country, but many of the markets of the Old World.   He lived to see educational institutions spring up anew where they had been paralyzed or destroyed by war.   He lived to help return the ballot to his comrades in arms from whom it had been taken, and he lived to be a potent agent in resisting Federal interference with State elections, and in taking from the statute books the laws which tended to give undue influence to Federal power in the elections of the people.

Although Mr. CRISP died so young, if we judge his life by its activities, its accomplishments, its successes, we may truly say he had a long and eventful public career.   I knew him well, having served with him during his whole term in Congress, and being connected with him in committee service at the time of his death.   He had a quick perception, a strong understanding, and a genial disposition.   Having lived in the same hotel with him for a considerable period, I knew his domestic life as well as his public.   The same gentleness in demeanor which characterized him when associating with his fellow-men he carried to the family circle intensified.   At the hearthstone, in the midst of his family, he was all that could be expected of the husband and father. As a member of this House, he was watchful and painstaking.   As its Speaker, when presiding over the House, he was courteous, ready, and firm.

Mr. Speaker, in the death of Mr. CRISP his State has lost an able and patriotic public servant, and our institutions a zealous advocate and a strong defender.   To his family every member who served with him and knew him will join in most heartfelt expressions of sympathy.

Mr. Speaker, the State of Kentucky, soon after the close

of the Mexican war, erected in the cemetery at her capital
a beautiful monument to her sons who fell in that war.
The gifted Theodore O'Hara recited at its dedication a poem
he composed for the purpose.   He was afterwards a comrade
in arms of Mr. CRISP, and I know not how better I can
express the feelings of his associates here from whom he
has been taken than by quoting the words of his comrade
spoken at that monument:

> Nor wreck, nor change, nor winter's blight,
>   Nor time's remorseless doom,
> Shall dim one ray of holy light
>   That gilds your glorious tomb.

ADDRESS OF MR. CUMMINGS.

Mr. CUMMINGS. Mr. Speaker, Tarquin, tyrant of Rome, once signified a desire to cut off the heads of his tallest nobles. If nobility of nature had been the standard, and CHARLES FREDERICK CRISP had lived under his dominion, he would certainly have been in danger. Nature had fashioned him with the greatest care. In the class for which she had designed him she had left a space very near the head of the list wherein he was to write his name. To fit him for it, however, his training was to be severe and varied. Man, soldier, jurist, he acted his part well; but it was as orator and statesman that he was to round up his career. The vicissitudes that intervened taught him endurance, faith, hope, and constancy, so that when he arrived at his destined service he was fitted for the tremendous encounters he was to endure.

He entered the lists with extreme modesty. His voice was low and soft, his demeanor graceful, his manner unobtrusive. He knelt at the shrine of the people, and rose knighted, the defender of their rights—a new champion in the lists. Among the throng he was hardly noticed, but he placed himself in front of his charge. When the poachers of power threatened his preserves, he started up—

> Not like the fox that shuns the snare,
> But lion of the hunt aware.

In the grapples that ensued he first leveled the approaches, that the contest might be fair. Then he stormed the citadel his adversary had set up. With herculean power and unyielding constancy he made every crevice feel his incisive assaults, and every salient the unabated force of his well-trained battery. When demolition ensued and all was over, he made the ruin effulgent with instructive lessons.

I might here close this sketch, satisfied that I had given an outline of the characteristics of this noble man, but he was my friend, at times my leader, always my instructor, and I feel it a duty on this occasion to fill it up with such observations on his career as my knowledge affords.

I shall speak of him with something of the suppressed emotion with which Antony struggled over the dead body of Cæsar, though in their lives there was little analogous, and in their death nothing whatever. Neither have I any motive, as the Roman had, for playing the cunning orator. To those who were here with him I need not say that his conduct was most noble under all circumstances; to those who were not here, I will say they have missed an exemplar whom they could have studied with advantage. Questions of tremendous import, of vast national importance, shook this Hall during his membership. Call to mind the great struggle over the force bill ; the lesser one over the McKinley bill. The first he opposed because he believed it a blow at the attributes of citizenship, sapping the foundations of our polity; the second because he deemed it the vicious outgrowth of a false political economy. All that party zeal, great research, and eminent ability could command clashed in these combats. At times the House swayed and tossed like a forest heaving to a tempest. When the storm had swept by and decorum had returned, such is the tenacity of party ties that alignments were found to be hardly affected.

How often, amid the wildest commotion, have I seen Mr. CRISP ride calm, dignified, and graceful, confident in the justice of his cause, spurred on by duty, and by his almost faultless diction, his earnest manner, and his all-sweeping logic soothe the struggling elements. Members might not agree with him, but they would listen. There was no malignity in him, nor even asperity. From his well-filled quiver he drew no poisoned arrow, for he knew that passion and judgment could have little fellowship, and he was earnest to convince.

His oratory was not overvehement. It flowed with regimental precision, close-ranked, animated, and confident. His bearing was always superb. I never knew him halt for a word or at fault for an illustration. When the situation warranted, he would light up the House with the liveliest display of humor. In attributes, in political tenets, and in his manner of illustration, he might not inaptly be called the John Bright of the American Commons.

His bouts with our distinguished Speaker, eminent for his talents and his audacity, were of thrilling interest.

Flashes of lightning and mutterings of thunder betokened the storm. It was like those intense situations we have so often seen upon the stage, where the future is threatening and the outcome dubious. It was not in the nature of either to give an inch of ground. When they had thus met in full career, and the strength and mettle of each had fully proved themselves on the other, they generally unlocked, if I may so express it, with something like defiant courtesy. Each had triumphed over the other for the Speakership; each could generously and truthfully say of the other: "Great let us call him, for he conquered me."

Many of us remember Mr. CRISP's contest for the Speakership. It was his ambition to preside over the House, of which he was so devoted a member. His party dominated

by an immense majority, and were privileged to caucus for
the prize. The contest was intense enough to unsettle
nerves not proof against disturbance. From first to last
he was threatened with defeat. Yet no ripple was observable in his even and well-sustained deportment. When
proclaimed victor, he received the honor with thanks,
emphasizing that he was conscious of the responsibility it
imposed and modestly showing he was confident he could
meet its claims. His address on taking the gavel was
a model of brevity and almost touching in simplicity.
Here it is :

GENTLEMEN OF THE HOUSE OF REPRESENTATIVES : For
the great honor you have conferred upon me I return you
heartfelt thanks.

I shall endeavor to discharge the duties of the office of
Speaker with courtesy, with firmness, and with absolute impartiality. Let us unite in the hope that our labors here may
result in the advancement of the prosperity, the honor, and
the glory of our beloved country.

The words "our beloved country" flowed into the speech
with as sweet a cadence as ever sprang from human heart
and fell from human lips. By unanimous vote the House
afterwards signified that he had fulfilled his highest
promise.

It was during his Speakership that his constancy was
severely tried. His highest ambition was to be a Senator
of the United States; but he desired to win the honor by
services faithfully rendered to his State and people. A
vacancy in the Senatorship occurred. The governor of
Georgia tendered it to him. He had but to accept it and
walk into the other house. He put it instantly aside to
serve out the term for which he had been chosen. Duty

chained him to the House, and that was a chain at which he never strained. In such estimation was he held by the people of his State that on the first occasion that offered itself they overwhelmingly designated him for the high position he had declined.

Such, Mr. Speaker, was your predecessor as I saw him and knew him in this House for many years. But there was a softer and far more tender shade to his character. It was his love for his home and family. I saw him and knew him in his typical Georgia home. I have conversed with him for hours while the mocking birds flooded the air with music and the sweet perfume of the cape jessamine was wafted to the porch. I have marked his devotion to an invalid wife, his tender affection for his children, and his generous care of old and tried servants emancipated in the war. I have sat at his table. Morning, noon, and night have I seen him bow his head and heard him ask God's blessing upon the food spread before him and his. It was a family united in love and affection—one in which the good old Southern term of endearment, "honey," was not forgotten. The children honored the father and the mother, and the parents honored the children. When the funeral procession passed the house, the words "His old home" were affixed in flowers above the gate. They had been placed there by his neighbors. It was thus he passed to a new home in the hereafter.

But his brilliant attributes will remain a resplendent memory, and when bereft of all human vanity, as I hope we may be, many of us, I am sure, as years go by, will declare with wholesome pride, "I was a member when Mr. CRISP was Speaker."

ADDRESS OF MR. HERMANN.

Mr. HERMANN. Mr. Speaker, it is related of a great historic character whose portrait was being painted that when the artist suggested he would eliminate from the picture a mole upon the face, the great man answered, "No; paint me as I am." Could the wish of our departed friend be known, it would be that his life, like the face of the portrait, should be represented just as it was. And well he could afford this wish. Sir, for nearly twelve years it was my privilege to be associated with CHARLES FREDERICK CRISP as a member of this Congress, and though differing with him on political lines, I esteem it a high privilege to unite with other associates in expressing this my tribute of respect, of love, and admiration for the life and character of this distinguished statesman. I speak of him as I always found him.

It seems but yesterday that we beheld in yonder chair the genial face and well-remembered form of him whose eulogy we now speak. Whether as the presiding officer of this House or as the unassuming and always courteous member on the floor, his presence was such as to invite the most kindly attention from his associates as well as from the onlookers in the gallery. Though one of the most devoted to any task undertaken by him, yet in the performance of that duty there was always shown a ready willingness to suffer interruption and with patience to answer either friend or opponent, and with equanimity to continue. A remarkable trait possessed by ex-Speaker CRISP was in his complete self-government. In all the debates in which he participated—and it was his lot while a member to participate in some of the most exciting controversies known to our annals—he maintained a manly self-possession, a placid, undisturbed, and unruffled temper, and a hold on his subject which eminently fitted him to occupy the trying position of leader of his party. It must have been a pleasure and a pride among his partisans to follow such a leader. There was an absence of egotism, of arrogance, of captiousness, of hauteur in his character. To the young members, more than all, will his memory in this respect be cherished.

The leader of a party in this House can, if his self-will so ordains, discourage and permanently impair the future of many a young member, while he can also encourage, aid, and incite him to his best efforts. Nothing so delighted Mr. Crisp as to rescue, by kindly suggestion or active aid, the embarrassed young member floundering in some trying debate or entangled in the parliamentary procedure of the House. Never was there a member of this body more approachable, more seemingly unconscious of high honors, and yet more dignified and more in place than he. The best test of his splendid character, however, was that which he soon developed in the Speaker's chair. In this exalted place the occupant too often abandons his previous cordial mannerism and at once assumes an air of austerity and lofty elevation above his fellows not justified by the dignity and authority of any office in this our republican form of government. With Speaker Crisp there was still retained the genial, lovable qualities which ever distinguished him before. He had grown no greater; his associates had grown no less. And yet he was the able, dignified, respected Speaker of the House of Representatives.

To the innumerable demands upon him for recognition he was courteous and patient—willing to hear the merits of the measure submitted, and then either granting, considering, or regretfully declining. Whatever was the answer, the member was made to feel that consideration was accorded him. His appeal had been kindly, respectfully heard. He could not complain. So sensitive was he to the feelings of his fellows, that never did he refuse a request that he did not suffer more pain than did the one denied. He never lost his control when Speaker. We all recall his superb bearing when presiding over the House when often wrought up to intense excitement over some political debate. It would seem as if the angry passions, the personal taunts, the criminations and recriminations on the floor, even to the extent of harsh reflection, fiery invective, and individual criticism hurled at the Speaker himself, would so unnerve and disturb him as to prompt retaliation upon his tormentors. Speaker CRISP rose grandly above this temptation. With a cool head and a firm gavel he ruled the storm and mastered it. When order was restored and the membership was again tranquil and the hot heads were cooling, not the slightest indication could be discerned in the face of the Speaker of the siege he had just passed through. He exemplified in the most practical manner and under the most trying circumstances the Scriptural injunction: "Let every man be swift to hear, slow to speak, slow to wrath."

And when at last in the revolution of parties another succeeded him in the chair, again he returned to the membership on the floor and resumed his duties as a Representative; he was still the same generous-hearted, considerate, self-sacrificing friend, associate, and member as he ever was.

With all the angry contentions which history will note as a part of his administration of this House, and which are still in vivid recollection, it is a refreshing boast, and confers imperishable luster upon his good name, that he exercised his powers as a Speaker in a fair and impartial manner as between the great parties on the floor, and that no stamp or stain suggestive of disrepute rests upon any public or private act during his long service as the trusted and distinguished representative of the people of his State.

Like the spire on some lofty cathedral seen at close view, when neither its true height nor its majestic proportions can be accurately measured, so is ex-Speaker CRISP, in according to him his just place in history in so brief a period after his death. His splendid life work will shine forth in even greater luster as time goes on, for then the mists which more or less obscure every active, ambitious genius, surrounded by enmities and personal antagonisms, will have faded away, and exposed to view the intrinsic worth and the perfect symmetry, the strength and beauty of this well-balanced life.

The light of our friend was extinguished while it was yet day—yea, at high noon. He was still in the midst of his usefulness, and no premonition pointed out the untimely end. The summons came, and the work was done. It is difficult to realize that this is true. Do we comprehend the uncertainty of life? Is it so frail? We hear the answer in the expiring breath and see it in the open grave. It leaves an admonition to us all: "Do thy work to-day; for thee there may be no to-morrow." May we not hope that if not here there may be that to-morrow in the celestial realms, "in that temple not made with hands, eternal in the heavens?"

Mr. Speaker, with these poor words in testimony of my high esteem for our departed associate, and in grateful remembrance of his noble, generous nature, I tenderly lay my sprig of acacia upon his honored grave.

ADDRESS OF MR. DINGLEY.

Mr. DINGLEY. Mr. Speaker, I made the acquaintance of CHARLES FREDERICK CRISP soon after he entered the Forty-eighth Congress as a Representative from Georgia. That acquaintance ripened into an intimate friendship, which continued till death removed him from the House of Representatives during the interval between the close of the first and the opening of the second session of the present Congress.

Notwithstanding our divergent political views often brought us into antagonism in debate, yet on all occasions he bore himself with such courtesy and kindliness of spirit, as well as ability and elevation of tone, that my respect for him personally and my admiration of his ability were increased. During my long service with Mr. CRISP, in which we were frequently on opposite sides of important and exciting political questions, nothing ever occurred to mar in the slightest degree our warm friendship and mutual regard.

For some time after entering Congress Mr. CRISP modestly refrained from active participation in the business and debates of the House, realizing as he did the importance of familiarizing himself first with the rules and methods of the House, so dissimilar in many respects from the practice of all of our State legislative bodies. Unlike many other parliamentary bodies, the House, partly from the necessity which exists in an assembly of so large a membership and partly because of its rapidly changing elements, pays little regard to courtesy in the conduct of its business, and grants very little to any member beyond what he is entitled to under its rules and practice.

I well remember the first time that Mr. CRISP forged to the front and demonstrated not only his ability as a legislator, but also his skill as a parliamentarian. It was on the occasion of the consideration and passage of the interstate-commerce bill, when the enforced absence of Judge Reagan, the chairman of the committee having that subject in charge, threw upon Mr. CRISP the responsibility of defending and guiding that important measure through the House in the face of a well-organized and determined opposition. This duty he performed with an ability, skill, and success which at once placed him among the leading members of the House—a rank which he subsequently maintained without difficulty.

When the Democratic party came into control of the House at the opening of the Fifty-second Congress, it was natural that Mr. CRISP's name should have been prominently mentioned for the Speakership, especially in view of the fact that while temporarily occupying the chair he had shown himself to be an expert parliamentarian and a successful presiding officer. But his nomination over older associates of larger experience and greater prestige was a recognition of his fitness for the high office of Speaker, which was shown to be well deserved. The ability and fairness with which he discharged the duties of this important and difficult position entitle Mr. CRISP to a high place among those great statesmen who have graced this high office, second only to the Presidency itself.

Mr. CRISP's mind was eminently logical and judicial. The possession of such a mind is absolutely essential to real success and usefulness in public service. In high public position men ruled by sentiment, who possess little logical power, little capacity to accurately weigh all sides of important questions, and especially to distinguish effects from causes, are always dangerous leaders, however sincere. Indeed, their power for mischief is only augmented by the earnestness which is sometimes born of inability to judicially weigh consequences. Mr. CRISP'S mind was so logical and judicial that he could see all around a question and avoid the errors and dangers of surface thinking.

Mr. CRISP'S position in the House was reached as much through his industry as through his ability. Indeed, no one achieves eminence either in public or private life except by persistent and well-directed work. There is no royal road to real and permanent success here or elsewhere. One who has carefully and thoroughly prepared himself to meet responsibilities is sooner or later needed. On the other hand, one who excuses himself from the labor required to make himself a master of his chosen line of study will never be able to keep to the front.

Mr. CRISP'S rapid rise from a humble condition to so high a position in the nation affords another illustration of the fact that in this land of the free merit is accorded recognition regardless of station or wealth. In spite of the effort of narrow minds to create the impression that there are classes in this country who secure privileges denied to the masses, the fact is that no class distinctions exist among our people, and that there is no distinction, no honor, no privilege which is not equally open to every citizen, however humble.

It is here in this Chamber, where Representatives from each of the forty-five States of the Union meet to consult with reference to the interests of this great Republic, that we feel as nowhere else the strength of the tie which binds together our seventy millions of people. Differ in opinion as we may, there rises above those differences the mutual regard engendered by the friendships here formed, and the feeling that we are fellow-citizens of a common country whose interest we desire to promote, and the heirs of a common heritage whose priceless blessings we desire to defend.

When, therefore, one of our number is removed by death, especially one who has been so long with us as has Mr. Crisp, we feel the separation not only as a national loss, but as a personal bereavement.

What we call death—the dissolution of the mysterious union of soul and body which characterizes life as discerned by our imperfect natural vision—is always an unwelcome, although inevitable, visitor. But when it comes to one who, like Mr. Crisp, was still young and in the height of his usefulness, the shock is intensified and the grief deepened. Happy is he who, when called to close his eyes on the scenes of earth and enter upon the life beyond, can meet this summons with a serene faith in Him who is over all and above all, as we doubt not was the case with our departed associate and friend.

ADDRESS OF MR. DE ARMOND.

Mr. DE ARMOND. Mr. Speaker, this hour is appropriately devoted to services in memory of a distinguished member of this body, lately with us, now gone to

> The undiscovered country, from whose bourn
> No traveler returns.

His life has been gracefully sketched by others far more familiar with it than I am, though I knew him quite well from service with him in the House of Representatives. I knew him somewhat also in the relations of friendship outside of the House. Of him it has been well said, because it has been truthfully said, that on the domestic side, as husband, father, friend, citizen, his life was not only without reproach, but admirable.

The career of CHARLES FREDERICK CRISP as a public man has been ably and fittingly outlined to-day before this audience and before the country. He himself painted the picture, and the lines have been but pointed out by those who have just engaged the attention of the House. A poor boy, he entered the Southern army from his Georgia home, and performed well the duties of a soldier "in times that tried men's souls." Emerging from the prison where he had been cast by the fortunes of war, with but little preparation except that which had been made in the rude school of the camp, he began the study of his chosen profession. How he rose in that profession from the stripling attorney at the bar to be solicitor-general, and soon became the chief presiding officer of the court; how by the suffrages of those who knew him well he was sent to this House, and how his legislative career, begun here and ended here, is honorable and illustrious—all

this is known to his associates and to the country too well
to need recital from me.

It may be worth while to inquire in what lay principally
the elements of the eminent Georgian's success. What was
there about him that elevated him above his fellows in a
body always distinguished for having within it many men
of great and commanding ability? How did he attain and
how did he retain leadership unquestioned within and over
a party difficult to lead and ever ready to throw aside leaders
and to choose new ones in their stead? That he was a man
of ability all know. But he led able men, who willingly
followed him. That he was a man of courage goes without
saying. But he had cheerful followers in men independent
as well as courageous, because they felt that he would
lead them aright. I believe that the one quality which
contributed mightily in giving him this ascendency in the
House—conceding to him great intellectual endowments—
lay in his amiable and lovable disposition. He won power
through his kindliness and retained it through kindness,
supplemented, of course, by tact, ability, and firmness.

His leadership was not self-imposed. To it he was called
voluntarily by his party associates, because they believed
he would lead in the course which it was right for them to
take—because it was not irksome to follow him—because
his leadership was so pleasant that it seemed but superior
fellowship.

Some men achieve greatness and command success in
ruling over other men by virtue of intellectual endowment
alone or by vast will power. While Mr. CRISP possessed
these great gifts of nature, he also possessed that sweet and
kindly disposition which attracted people to him, which
made people love to be associated with him, and which
preserved his sway over the minority, as it is now—over

the majority as it was for a time—as perhaps the sway of no other man of his party will be established or maintained in this House in many a day to come. He has gone; gone to return to these Halls no more. I can not add to his fame, nor could I detract from it. His life work is known; it is approved by those who knew it best. His career was indeed a remarkable one; and if he had not died in his prime, there is no guessing how many new triumphs of statesmanship might be placed to his credit.

What a proud thing it is, Mr. Speaker, for a man starting poor and working his way without extraneous aid to rise by the power of his own personality, by his intellect and lovable qualities, to the high position which Mr. CRISP reached, and which you, too, twice gained; an official position second only to one other in the world; a place which, well filled—filled by intellect, courage, courtesy, kindness, impartiality—is often in a lifetime even higher than any official station not occupied by a man possessing the same estimable qualities of the head and of the heart. Then, true indeed it is that Mr. CRISP'S was a life upon whose bright, clean, glorious story we may dwell with profit to ourselves and to those who are to come after us.

Leadership is not necessarily sought or coveted. It is generally born in the man. Sometimes it is acquired by a man's own zeal, and sometimes it is thrust upon a man. However, men of superior ability naturally aspire to leader-ship; not a few attain it without real merit. But those who, because of qualities inherent in themselves, retain leader-ship over followers possessed of the power to depose them— these few are men born to lead, as others are born to follow.

Perhaps the proudest tribute to the memory of the departed statesman whose death we mourn is that he retained his ascendency over men not so much by virtue of special effort as through the warm feeling, akin to affection, which his sunny disposition and native kindliness awakened in his associates, so that they felt themselves honored in honoring him.

The loss to Speaker CRISP's party and to his country is almost irreparable. While we of the minority have many able and strong men among us, yet attention does not turn to anyone in particular as being peculiarly fitted, as he was, for the post of leader. At least, no one stands out, to the exclusion of the others, like Mr. CRISP did, as the proper leader here of the forces of the Democracy.

I esteem it a privilege, Mr. Speaker, that, as a member of this body, I have beheld two great parliamentary leaders, one upon either side of the Chamber, each superb in his own way, marshal their respective forces, now for attack, now for defense. I do not expect again in life, though my years be prolonged to great length, to find their equals in ability to lead and govern their fellow-partisans in parliamentary warfare. But could either have led so successfully the forces which followed the other?

Often we think and say that those who die in their prime are taken prematurely. Of course, to family and friends, to love and hope and pride, the shock comes most rudely when the blast of death has blown where, it would seem, the blush of life ought to continue. But, after all, when you consider the fame in years to come of a man whose life is full of good deeds and grand achievements, as was Mr. CRISP's—looked at in the light of history—is it an unmixed misfortune in the annals of the world that such a one goes down when the sun is at high noon, instead of lingering on the stage of action, often superfluous, until the long and ever-lengthening shadows from the west are falling upon him?

Yet there is no doubt that if Mr. CRISP had been spared he would long have been one of the greatest members of the Senate, whose doors were open for him to enter; no doubt that had he lived he would have gone from honor to honor; no doubt that his fame and usefulness would have grown and expanded, no matter how rich the honors and deeds to his credit when the dread destroyer overtook him.

His career is hardly matched in the legislative history of the country. At least there are few to lay side by side with it; and with his honors full upon him, in the full possession of his magnificent abilities, surrounded by his beloved family and cherished friends, his warm heart ceased to beat and his great intellect was transferred to another scene of action. Long will his memory live in the hearts and in the minds of all who knew him. Long will his services to his country be remembered gratefully by those who justly appreciate them, kindly even by those who believe he was wrong politically, because, above all things, he was an amiable man in high station, who as nearly avoided the giving of offense to any, and as uniformly treated all with consideration, kindness, and generosity, as anyone of whom we have a record or anyone whom we may ever expect to meet.

Mr. Speaker, in contemplation of these sad events, which are occurring daily—for death is almost as old in the world as life; with the centuries full of life and death, and death, like birth, marking every hour and every minute of every day—we are brought, over and over, time and time again, to the strange, alway sold, and ever fresh reflections which will spring up when we gaze into the open grave, when we view the cold and lifeless clay which so recently was the mortal shelter of the departed spirit. Filled with that awe which the ages have not been able to banish, which pervades generation after generation, we solemnly ask, Whither has the spirit gone that lately tenanted this clay? What is there of existence beyond this world? Or is this all? Is this the end? We can not see through the veil just a little way before us, but thick enough to cloud the sight. Faith and Hope alone light up the gulf; alone give promise for the future.

Our friend has gone. His memory is with us, enshrined in our hearts. By his example we hope to profit. But again the query presses for answer, "If a man die, shall he live again?" The abandoned clay is in the churchyard at Americus, under sweet flowers, with the soft Southern sky bending over all. But the spirit! What of it? Is that, which was so much, nothing now—vanished, dissolved, annihilated, as though it never was? Did its existence terminate with the life of the body? Whatever vainglorious philosophers may say, man rebels at the suggestion that there is nothing beyond the grave. The hope, sometimes clung to in desperation, sometimes cherished in brightest anticipation, that there is a hereafter, and that men, though they die, yet live in that hereafter—we will not give that up. No philosophy, even if ripened in ages of calm reasoning, can banish it. It springs as an inheritance of humanity, as an instinct in the soul of every human being that breathes. We believe—our hopes, our affections, all that we hold near and dear in life, admonish us to believe, constrain us to believe—that our friend has not perished, but that in a higher and nobler sphere this great intellect, this tender, loving spirit shall flourish and expand, and achieve new triumphs and perform new deeds of glory and of grace while countless ages roll on into eternity.

ADDRESS OF MR. DINSMORE.

Mr. DINSMORE. Mr. Speaker, in the presence of gentlemen here who were so much nearer to CHARLES FREDERICK CRISP, who were so fortunate as to have a more extended acquaintance with him, a closer relation, a longer term of service, I approach with diffidence and hesitation the honorable privilege which has been extended to me to speak in commemoration of a great man who made his life a part of the illustrious history of this House. It is not for me to criticise his great character. I leave that to those more capable of the task. I only desire, Mr. Speaker, to place upon record the humble tribute of one who had an acquaintance and friendship with him through a few years, but who, during that whole time, learned to honor, admire, and love him more and more.

It is at all times a delicate and a responsible undertaking to speak here for the permanent record upon the life and character of one who has been a member of this House. Men are too prone to run into extravagant expression, to magnify the virtues of the dead as well as disparage the merits of the living. What is said upon these occasions should be not only just to the dead, but faithful to truthful history. I fain would, in the few sentences which I shall speak to-day, do so as if in presence of the conscious spirit of our departed friend, knowing that he would have me give utterance to no sentiment that is not justified by his own life. Nor have I sought for information upon the detailed incidents of his history, preferring to put into words the impressions that association with the man have made upon me, and to stop there.

Duty does not demand of us to enlarge upon or even to

refer to foibles of character; but, on the other hand, it is required of us that in the things we say we shall deal fairly and honestly with ourselves and with the dead.   Therefore I shall endeavor to restrain my expressions within the bounds of temperate speech, within the limits which I believe would be indorsed by our great leader if he could be present and hear what is said of him.

Mr. Speaker, every man's life, in a narrower or wider sense, is an ideal for other men.   Whether it be lowly or exalted, whether it be humble or great, there is among every man's associates some person who will look to him as an exemplar of his own conduct, who will find in him something worthy of imitation; and it is pleasant to think there are few men who do not thus exercise an influence for good upon mankind.   The greatest good of a great life is its influence upon society.   In the aspirations of early youth the boy selects some great character of history and tries to fashion himself upon that model, to build himself up to that level.   What a grand figure have we here to inspire the ambition, the fortitude, the patriotism, and the integrity of American youth, aye, and of American manhood!

Mr. Speaker, I have had the honor, in the short time I have served in the House, to be associated with Mr. CRISP as Speaker of the House in one Congress and as the acknowledged leader of the minority in another.   In every relation, in every emergency, in every situation it has appeared to me that he arose to the full stature of great manhood and capability of dealing with the difficult tasks that confronted him. As Speaker of the House, as leader upon the floor, as a citizen in private life, he was always thoughtful and dignified, firm and unyielding in adherence to principle, and bold and fearless in defense of it, yet withal kind, gentle, courteous, and considerate.   As Speaker, he was easy of access to every member of the House, even though the humblest, newest, most obscure member that had come into it—easy of approach, and always having words of encouragement for those who sought to make themselves useful in the great House over which he had the honor to preside.

I have no doubt that each one who came into the House while he was Speaker has pleasant memories of his own experience and of the words of counsel he has given, and we cherish in our minds tender memories never to be effaced. He was gentle as a woman, simple in his demeanor, yet always calm, dignified, self-possessed, strong, and great. As leader of his party on the floor, he controlled his forces more by inspiring them with love and confidence than with fear of discipline. He was tolerant of the impulsive ardor of the inexperienced, of the "vaulting ambition" of youth that in this forum so often "doth o'erleap itself," and gave full value to the usefulness of every member.

But, Mr. Speaker, it was in the fury of polemic tempest that this man rose superior to his fellows. The louder shrieked the winds of passion, the higher mounted the surging waves of partisan animosity, the greater appeared the man, the more capable of battling for his cause and of representing the issues for which he stood. This was one of the characteristics of the man—that he shone best under the greatest difficulties—and it seemed to require great and critical situations to bring out his intellectual qualities and his great power of leadership. And he has challenged the admiration not only of this side, but of that, and the whole country, for his great ability in performing the stern duties of presiding officer of this unruly House.

It perhaps accords with common observation that simplicity, gentleness, kindness, and unostentation are almost universally characteristics of the truly great man. Consciousness of acknowledged superiority, of security in a position of leadership, and of general approbation and respect generates charity toward rivals and consideration for opposition, and causes a great mind to contemn pompous parade and vulgar display, the artifice and the trick of the demagogue. Our departed friend despised all things of this character. He always drove straight for the mark, and by the ponderous power of logic and reason and appeal to honor and patriotism he hewed his way to the accomplishment of his great purpose, always unyielding, brave, and courageous, yet generous to opposition, and never forgetting to be courteous to all and considerate of all.

The privilege was accorded me of a slight glimpse into his domestic life, and it was there, Mr. Speaker, that the beautiful attributes of his character were brought most prominently into view. A devoted husband, a kind, gentle, and affectionate father, his faithful wife adored him and his children hung upon him as the tendrils of the vine entwine themselves about the body of the sturdy oak. Coming out of the war almost a youth, with no inheritance save a soldier's honorable name won in a cause that was lost, with no possession other than a tattered uniform and the blood, brain, and brawn that God had given him, he started out to make for himself a place in society and in his country's history. At the threshold there was linked with his life a young, confiding, loving woman, who in the flush of youthful affection defied the will of parental authority and joined herself to him to march by his side through the highways and byways and the uncertain incidents of this world.

When the time came, Mr. Speaker, when the blush of beauty had faded from her cheek and the form he loved in its youthful beauty had been wrenched in the cruel tortures

of rheumatism, there was no lessening of the love which he
gave to her in the beginning, but with stronger and greater
attachment he stood by her side, and when she held out her
crippled hand the love light mounted to his eyes and he
was wont to say: "But I will be your hand. You shall
walk upon my feet." Those hands and those feet, Mr.
Speaker, never failed her, but were ever present to perform
their affectionate offices. A beautiful intimacy existed
between him and his children. Often have I looked up
with admiration from my table at the hotel where we all
lived, when father and son—that son whom a loving people
have sent here to fill the vacant chair caused by the relentless hand of death, honoring both father and son in the
deed and themselves as well—would walk in side by side,
sometimes hand in hand, often arm in arm, before the
assembled guests, utterly unconscious that any were looking with admiration upon the beautiful comradeship which
existed between the two. And there are not many things
more beautiful than confidence and fellowship between
father and son, nor anything better calculated to impress
the son or lead him upward and onward in an honorable
life and to an enviable old age.

But, Mr. Speaker, in the midst of his honors, in the
very zenith of his usefulness and his splendid life, the scythe
of the reaper has mown him down. He has left his foot-
prints upon the highways of our nationality; he has
engraved his name upon the tablets of his country's history;
he has left behind him a name to be emulated and honored,
and he has carried with him the respect of his enemies, the
admiration and affection of his friends, the devotion of his
family, the confidence and esteem of all; and what more,
Mr. Speaker, can any man claim for himself upon going
out from this world?

ADDRESS OF MR. BUCK.

Mr. BUCK. Mr. Speaker, I had hoped to be able to add in my best voice to the tributes that are paid to-day to the honored dead. But the elements seem against me; and I do not know whether I shall be able even to make myself heard.

The propriety, Mr. Speaker, that some one young in membership in this House should say something of that great public servant whose memory and whose deeds are here commemorated must be the apology for my presuming to add my humble voice to these tributes. When Hamlet is challenged to the duel with Laertes, Osrick says to him: "You are not ignorant of what excellence Laertes is." Hamlet replies: "I dare not confess that, lest I should compare with him in excellence; but to know a man well were to know himself."

There is therefore in these things a semblance, if not a substance, of self-praise which under any circumstances would make me modest in speaking of the great dead whom we honor here to-day.

I anticipated, however, the situation. I knew that members of this House who knew him better than I and were better able to speak his praises and display the beauties of his character would precede me, and I would be relieved of anything more than the expression of that impression which I gladly and truthfully convey and which it was my good fortune to imbibe from him during the short period that it has been my happiness to know him. It has perhaps been my good luck that in this very short period I

have learned to know more of him than happens in the
average intercourse between members of this House. And,
without repeating what has been said, I can only say that,
perhaps by operation of that inexplicable intuition by which
soul communicates with soul, I received the impressions of
that greatness of character, that firmness of mind, that
consistency of purpose, that devotion to duty which distinguished CHARLES FREDERICK CRISP and which language
can not exaggerate. I will ask the privilege, in view of the
fact that the memory of the dead and his deeds are on record,
to pronounce a few reflections incident to this service which
perhaps also convey their lesson.

I have heard criticised—I may say ridiculed and con-
demned—the practice not only of the Houses of Congress,
but of courts and other public bodies, to spend hours like
these in eulogies upon the dead. Well, it is in the nature
of things. There is evil as there is good. The scoffer is
at hand to tread upon the heels of the reverent. The jester
and the clown are by in the motley mystery of human life
to mix their colors in the garments of wisdom and of dignity. But these things come not from men who see "books
in the running brooks, sermons in stones, and good in everything."

I am the spirit that denies—

says the arch scoffer—

Part of the part am I; once all, in primal night—
Part of the darkness which brought forth the light.

Why, sir, that is the struggle, the epic of man's redemp-
tion, to overcome the spirit of denial and survive godlike
in the prevalence of truth. And truth prevails and is evidenced to-day when this House of Representatives turns
aside from its usual business and from its public service to
lay the flowers of tribute upon the tomb of the departed

dead.   As we look down the ages and let pass before the
view the toils and the struggles, the failures and the successes, the lights and the shades of human character and
effort; and above all, when we look into our own souls, and
try to square ambition with achievement, desire with con-
summation, hope with possibility—aye, all the contradic-
tions and paradoxes of conduct and aspiration—we do rise
from the contemplation with the conviction that through
all there is a higher destiny.   And even in the blankness of
despair and the tragedy of hopelessness, we exclaim with
Hamlet, in the ecstacy and exultation of our souls—

What a piece of work is man! How noble in reason! how infinite in
faculties! in form and moving, how express and admirable! in action,
how like an angel! in apprehension, how like a god!

Are not these thoughts justified when we recall that
majestic, that self-controlled, that courageous, that manly
figure that drew by his magnetic look the attention of his
followers and the admiration, if not the approbation, of
his opponents?

Public service should, as a principle in our country, be
always commended.   Few men enter politics from purely
selfish motives.   They do not find, if they enter from selfish
motives, what they seek.   They soon find that it is a service
and a sacrifice, not a gathering of fruits; and whatever the
original motive may be with which public men begin to
develop themselves, there is always at the bottom the sentiment of patriotism, a desire and an ambition to serve our
fellow-men, to be workers in the field of progress and of
good toward our country.   The wholly selfish man rarely
troubles himself about public life.   He nurses his personal
comfort, and concerns himself no further about the law and
the liberty of the land than is necessary to protect his own

rights and the pursuit of happiness as he understands it. Happily for the human race and happily for this great country and the people of the United States, mankind stands vindicated in the high shrines of the temples of duty and devotion. It awes the scoffer into ineffectual retreat. It shoves by the selfish. The history of man and human progress is an eternal story of sacrifice, devotion, and of self-denial.

We know where in this struggle the departed dead stood; and let us reflect, as has been said, that if he does not take his place among those meteoric successes which come from genius, yet he ranks among those men whose names live in history, not by the noise which they have made for themselves only, as the Cæsars and the Napoleons, but in the rhythm of those gentle streams and strains that flow from their heart's sympathy for the welfare of mankind. We admire genius; but genius is the gift of God rather than the virtue of attainment. We look up to a Homer, a Dante, a Shakespeare, and a Goethe as to the inspired of God; but when, in solemn judgment, we pass on the merits of men in the light of their practical service and usefulness, the civilized acclaim goes up to the jurist and the soldier, the philosopher and the legislator, the inventor and the reformer, as the pillars on which the temple of development is erected. Behold Solon and Leonidas, Guttenberg and Luther, Franklin and Washington! And, Mr. Speaker, if not among these men as leaders, still among them, as a class, we place the name of Mr. CRISP.

Not to repeat a threadbare quotation (if Shakespeare ever can be threadbare), he was of that robust directness which is always honest and honorable; firm as a rock and candid as the light. Aggressive, perhaps, at times to the point of severity, he was ever consistent and conscientious. Self-reliant without ostentation, fixed to his purpose like the northern star, his ambition cast in the high mold of patriotism and general welfare, he will hold his place, all in all, in that rank of men of giant and heroic mold, of all the elements of manhood well compact, of which the majestic Brutus will ever be the literary and historic type.

Mr. Speaker, it is grateful to render these testimonials of affection and approval to the departed dead. It is grateful to live with them—to remember them, as it were—in the pure atmosphere of spiritual conception, gathering the good they have done into tangible shape as examples for emulation and pledges for the growth and happiness of the future of mankind. So with our honored dead. However inadequate our tributes may be—while what he leaves behind him in the memory of his perfect character and patriotic service is already secure for all time—they give vital movement to the good which he accomplished; and its present influence will go out at once to the American people, that they may know and feel how glorious a thing is the perfect American citizen.

In this great republic of humanity, where in every village churchyard the willow shades the graves of sovereign masters; where every—even the humblest—heart may swell with the passions of a destiny grander and nobler than the majesty of kings, public virtue is a public need and public recognition a duty and a consecration.

The republics of antiquity made their great men and their heroes gods, not only to honor the dead, but to incite the living to emulate their illustrious careers. The great people of these United States, for once and ever, should turn back the slander that republics are ungrateful. Let them ever recognize greatness and reward service, honor character, and glorify achievement. With that will come regard for constituted authority and reverence for law, which mean peace and order. So shall we develop the perfect citizenship and consummate the highest aims of self-government ; so shall we adorn our liberties and make sacred our sense of justice ; and so, Mr. Speaker, and so best, will be served and honored the glorious dead, whose strong arms were their country's and whose heart-throbs were the aspirations of humanity. Among these, transfigured in the light of immortality, will stand Mr. CRISP. He will live long in the affections of his people, and the virtues of his patriotism and the record of his services will shine out among the brightest in the uplifting spheres of human liberty and the unmatched heavens of American citizenship. Thus the living render their devotions, that the dead may be at rest.

> Such honors Ilium to her hero paid,
> And peaceful sleeps the mighty Hector's shade.

ADDRESS OF MR. COOPER.

Mr. COOPER. Mr. Speaker, I well remember the first day that I ever saw CHARLES FREDERICK CRISP. It was during the preparations for the opening of the Fifty-third Congress. He stood apparently in all the vigor of manhood's prime, surrounded by the leaders of his party in this House, full of life and hope, of vitality and courage, yet receiving all with that cordiality, that easiness of access, that charm of manner that was characteristic of the man, and was but the outward reflection of an inward kindliness of heart.

It seems but yesterday. It is but a few short years as days are counted, and yet within that space of time we have made much history. We have seen many hopes fade, we have witnessed many misfortunes; but nothing sadder than the event that draped that desk in mourning and cut short in mid course the high career of Mr. CRISP.

Truly, Mr. Speaker, these things are beyond human understanding. He was surrounded by a loving family, by troops of friends. He had the esteem and good wishes of thousands of his fellow-countrymen. He stood just upon the threshold of yet further official preferment and honor from that great State that has so often honored him and that he has so honored, when, at the very noon time of his life, when his sun seemed to be at the very zenith, suddenly it declined and went out.

Sir, it is not merely an individual loss that we lament here to-day. It is the loss to a great party and the loss to his country. When the leader of one of the great parties of this country, full of experience, yet in the prime of life, full of capability and patriotism, of vigor and of force, and yet conservative as Mr. CRISP was, is taken away, his loss is at any time a calamity in such a country as ours. But a such a day as this, when dissensions and discords distract us; when, look where we will, we see but threatening clouds; when all circumstances call upon us to realize the need of those high attributes which the great State of Georgia— which he represented, and where I had the honor to be born—has engraved upon her coat of arms as the chief sup- porters of the governmental fabric—justice, wisdom, and moderation—how great is our loss in such a man! I had hoped much from the wisdom and the moderation of Mr. CRISP. He was never a theorist or an extremist. He hoped for the perpetuity of his party, which he regarded as one of the instruments of good government, and he loved his coun- try. With his wide knowledge of public men, with a high career before him, with the open field of opportunity, I looked for years of usefulness and honor, in which he would have not only advanced his own reputation, but in which he would have been of most material assistance to his people, to the preservation of his party, and to securing the prosperity and welfare of his country. But, sir, that, too, has passed.

When I rose here, it was not with the idea that anything I could say would be of any consequence to his fame or add aught to him. He has written his own memorial in the records of this House and on the pages of his country's history. When I was asked to assist in these services, I felt it to be a high honor. Others who have been much longer here have dwelt upon his qualities and upon his course in this House. I can add nothing to that; but to one charac- teristic it is peculiarly appropriate that I should render my testimony. I came to the Fifty-third Congress a new member, comparatively a young man, and I know that everyone who participated in that Congress, and who so came here, will join me in the tribute which I pay to Mr. CRISP when I say that his generous hand, guided by that kindly heart, held wide open always, when it was possible, the gates of opportunity to the inexperienced and to those who could do naught for him, but for whom he could do so much.   It is a pleasure to me indeed to-day to be able to testify in some small degree my gratitude for that constant kindness.   He has gone beyond the reach of our words, but he is not dead.   "As the tall ship, whose lofty prow shall never stem the billows more," he has merely sought a haven of rest.   No man is dead while he is borne in affectionate or grateful remembrance, and, Mr. Speaker, Mr. CRISP will live long in the hearts of many.

ADDRESS OF MR. SWANSON

Mr. SWANSON. Mr. Speaker, a great public career has ended. One of the foremost public men of our country has been stricken down. One of the greatest parliamentary leaders of this age is no more. One of the shining lights of this House, whose splendid achievements have and will ever shed luster upon it, is no longer with us. The recognized leader of this side of the House, who counseled and directed us, has departed and left us to mourn a loss which is irreparable. A great heart, warm, generous, kind, and magnetic, no longer pulsates. A mind, clear, strong, and masculine, of great depth and grasp, no longer gives us its scintillations of thought. A tongue of great eloquence and power, which has so often stirred and swayed this House, is now silent in death. A life in which can be traced much of shadow and shine, much of privation and much of triumph, inspiring in its success over difficulties, admirable in development and attained proportions, has terminated, and we to-day pause in our deliberations to pay merited tribute to and to do reverence to one who has left behind him such a life.

I rise to deliver no elaborate eulogium—others have done that—but simply on behalf of my State and myself to place a modest chaplet of love and admiration upon the grave of CHARLES FREDERICK CRISP. Virginia has ever felt toward Mr. CRISP an affection akin to that entertained for one of her own distinguished sons. When the storms of the late civil war burst over this country, Mr. CRISP, then a youth in Virginia, enlisted in one of her regiments, and became a gallant and brave soldier in defense of her soil. These years of his, consisting of triumphs and privations, of glory and disappointments, are interwoven with the history of Virginia and her sons. No section rejoiced more than she at his increasing success and fame; now in mourning his loss she is second to none.

Mr. Speaker, Emerson, one of the greatest of American thinkers and writers, has said:

A man's fortunes are the fruits of his character. A man's friends are his magnetisms.

How fully is this truth illustrated in the life of Mr. CRISP. His life was one crowned with great fortune, blessed with friends innumerable. Thus we find in him a sterling, honest character, a strong masculine mind, blended with a warm, generous, magnetic heart. To be great and to be loved as much as admired, to wield great power and influential leadership, with each day bringing an increasing devotion, indicates the possession of the highest order of intellect, the very best qualities of heart. Mr. CRISP possessed all this. No leader ever enjoyed in a greater degree the combined confidence and affection of his followers than Mr. CRISP did that of his party associates in this House. We all felt he was our individual friend and our matchless party leader. We shall ever hold his personal traits in loving remembrance, his public career in proud recollection. Who can ever forget that straight, strong form, that handsome face, that unfailing courtesy, that warm grasp of the hand, that genial, pleasant smile, that carried sunshine and happiness wherever he went?

Mr. Speaker, Mr. CRISP will ever be remembered for his participation in exciting scenes and debates in this House which have become historical. Our memory and the imagination of our successors, aided by tradition and history, will ever recall his wonderful powers as a parliamentary debater. With a voice at times slightly tinged with hesitancy, but clear, strong, and resonant, with a presence pleasing and attractive, with thoughts pertinent and incisive, a repartee quick and pointed; cool, calm, and collected amid the greatest excitement and passion, he was well equipped for the rough-and-tumble debates of this House, and it was in these that he showed himself preeminently great. This House has had few if any Speakers superior to him. He will be classed among its greatest and most noted. As Speaker, he presided with dignity and grace, transacted business promptly, decided points of order quickly, was firm and decisive. He was courteous, deferential, and fair to his political opponents. His whole public life is without spot or blemish. For four years as Speaker, an office in responsibility and power second only to that of the Presidency, he practically controlled the legislation of this country. He exercised the vast powers thus placed in his hands with prudent care, patriotically, and conscientiously, for what he conceived the best interest of his country. No corrupt job, no vicious, no unjust legislation ever received countenance from him.

Mr. Speaker, the life of Mr. CRISP is instructive. It comes like an inspiration to the poor boy, situated as he was, possessed of high yearning, yet confronted with poverty and difficulties, and tells him not to despair, but to build high the pedestal of his ambition. It teaches the ambitious that great success and permanent fame can only come to those who have clean hands, pure hearts, and patriotic motives. It proclaims how a legislator can and should close his ears to the seductions of the rich few, but can and should listen to the heart beat of toiling and struggling humanity.

ADDRESS OF MR. LACEY.

Mr. LACEY. Mr. Speaker, it is fitting that in the hurry and bustle of public affairs we should pause for a time and remember that all men are but mortal. The painful truth is thrust upon us from time to time as one of our associates falls out of the ranks.

Our friend, whose death brings us again face to face with the great problem that we all in time must solve, had risen high among his fellow-men. There is but one official place among his countrymen higher than that to which he climbed.

The Speakership, it has been often said, is the second place in this country in rank, if its power and influence be considered. The General Commanding the Army holds a more desirable place, because his office tenure is for life. The Chief Justice and Vice-President both take a higher rank theoretically, but the actual second place in the nation is that of the Speakership of the House of Representatives.

All revenue bills must originate in the House, and that body in the most direct degree represents the people. Their term of office is so short that its members are kept in constant touch with the people. A member of Congress is elected in November and does not, except in case of an extra session, take his seat until thirteen months after his election. He has hardly entered upon his duties until the selection of his successor begins to be agitated. In every official act he is face to face with his constituents.

The supreme position in a body of this kind is a leadership of the people themselves.

The House contains 357 members, and so large a body would be hopelessly inefficient and unwieldy if great power were not lodged in the Speaker's hands. He selects the committees and designates the seniority of their members and even appoints their chairmen. The committee is the workshop of the House, and no member can accomplish any results in his legislation unless he is assigned to committees in which he is able to perform his chosen work. He is like an actor in a play who has been given a walking part if he is placed upon committees where he has no opportunities for action, or in a line of work for which he is unprepared or to which he is unadapted.

The Speaker may, in the very beginning of a session of Congress, place a member where he may have opportunities, or so shelve him that he can accomplish nothing. This power extends to the minority membership as well as to those of the dominant party, and its influence is felt in every Congressional district in the Union.

But the power of the Speaker does not end here. He has the right to recognize members upon the floor and he may refuse to do so, and there is no redress. He can shape the course of legislation by giving opportunities to present the measures which he may approve. He is the chairman of the Committee on Rules, and this committee is composed of only five members, three of whom are of his own party. In selecting this committee he is practically enabled to bring forward any measure he may wish at almost any time, and the House can only prevent action by voting against the present consideration of the proposed measure.

Usually less than 10 per cent of all the proposed legislation in Congress is ever considered at all, owing to the enormous amount of business brought before that body.

This being the case, of necessity there must be a power and discretion resting somewhere by which the necessary business may be selected and considered out of the great mass of the measures introduced.   In the last Congress presided over by Mr. CRISP, 11,797 Senate and House bills were presented, and of these, 563 public and 593 private bills were enacted into laws.   Congress is generally entitled to more credit for the bills that it permits to die than for any other part of its work, so that the failure to consider bills is not usually an evil.   The power of the Speaker to prevent legislation is therefore a most important function.   The Speaker has the power to delegate his authority temporarily as presiding officer by selecting some other member for that purpose, and he also names the chairmen of the Committee of the Whole from time to time.

New members are apt to chafe at first because of the extraordinary powers of the presiding officer, but upon further service they realize that in so large an organization, having such a multiplicity of important business, the system of which they complained at first is essential to the transaction of the business of the country.

A Congress which must consider the appropriation and expenditure of from eight hundred to a thousand millions of dollars in two years must be under a complete system of rules, or they could not have sufficient time for their duties. But, with all his power, the Speaker is still the servant of the House, and constantly recognizes that fact.   Strong and able men are almost invariably selected for this place, and they are almost always strong partisans.

The responsibility of Congress to the people, and the fact that the Speaker himself must also stand for reelection in the near future, places him in a position where he must not abuse his power.   He not only is in a place where his own future and that of most of the members is in his hands, but the future of his party is also largely dependent upon the wisdom and skill with which he exercises his important prerogatives. He can shape the course of his party with almost as much certainty as the President himself.

The speakership of the English House of Commons, on the other hand, is not political, but is rather judicial in its character. The ministry upon the floor of that chamber are responsible to the House and to the country, and the Speaker's duties are more like those of a mere presiding officer in a court of justice. ·

All who have seen service in this House will readily concede to our presiding officer a place second only to that of the President of the United States.

Mr. CRISP's first term of office followed immediately after the Fifty-first Congress, where the powers of the office had been so fully demonstrated by Speaker Reed. The attention of the country had been called in an unusual degree to the Speaker's chair, and Mr. CRISP took the place at a time when the people looked upon the office with a full appreciation of its importance. Having personally assailed the prerogatives of the position when in the minority, he was embarrassed in his first term by his own utterances in debate. But in his second term, when his party was distracted by questions which almost threatened its existence, he was compelled to exercise to the uttermost the very powers that he had so severely criticised, even adopting, in a modified form, the same rules that had given a nickname to his Republican predecessor.

Speaker CRISP was too great a man to allow the reins to slip from the hands of his party in the mere effort to be consistent. He recognized the necessity of adopting methods which would enable the dominant party to enact the measures for which that party must answer to this country. Those who served with him knew how ably he conducted himself in the most trying and difficult positions in which he had been placed.

While the Speaker's chair is the seat of influence, yet in a stirring popular assembly it is the object of constant partisan assault, and he whose memory we commemorate to-day in turn was the attacking and the assaulted party. But it is one of the pleasant features of parliamentary life that partisan foes are so often personal friends. Mr. Crisp loved a good fighter, and was a hard hitter himself.

His career is a striking example of the possibilities of life in our Republic.

In the Fifty-third Congress Galusha A. Grow was sworn in by Speaker Crisp as a member at large from the State of Pennsylvania. This was an impressive act, and brought into comparison two great periods in the history of our people. In 1861 Mr. Grow was chosen as the war-time Speaker of this House. Mr. Crisp was then a young lieutenant in a company of Confederate infantry, and the civil war was raging with all its fury.

In 1864 Mr. Crisp was a prisoner of war, and was not released until after hostilities had ceased, in June, 1865. Now, after thirty years, the veteran statesman from Pennsylvania returned again to the Halls of Congress, and the young lieutenant of 1861 had become the Speaker of the House of Representatives of our reunited country and administered the oath of office to his predecessor, the ex-Speaker of that Congress which had enacted the measures to prosecute the war.

Who could say in the face of such an event as this that we have not laid aside the prejudice and bitterness of the struggle of 1861?

And as a citizen of Iowa I wish to lay a tribute upon the tomb of the gallant Georgian, remembering only that we were both in a higher sense fellow-citizens of the United States of America.

My first service in this House was on the Elections Committee with our deceased friend, in the heated and stormy sessions of the Fifty-first Congress. Election contests are proverbial for the partisan feeling that they engender.

Mr. CRISP on these occasions showed himself a sturdy partisan, and it was in these controversies that he won the influence with his party associates that brought him to the Speaker's chair in the succeeding Congress. He was a good parliamentarian, subtle, quick-witted, and always ready for any occasion that might arise, and his party friends rallied around him with that instinct which teaches men to involuntarily recognize a leader.

In his private relations he was an agreeable and pleasing gentleman, and made friends on both sides of this Chamber at a time when the political forces were nearly equally divided and when party feeling ran high. But all his conflicts of the past—in the tented field, at the bar, on the hustings, and in the Halls of Congress—are ended. Already pointed out by common consent for a certain election to a seat in the Senate, he was struck down in the very zenith of his career, mourned by those who knew him, of all parties.

It was a graceful and gracious act on the part of the generous people of his old district to elect his son and namesake to fill the seat which his death had rendered vacant, and this pleasing circumstance showed how strong a hold he had upon the constituency which he had so long represented, and how fully they appreciated the beauty and purity of his private life and domestic relations.

The applause with which members of all parties greeted the son upon taking the oath of office showed in what kindly remembrance they held the sire.

ADDRESS OF MR. BELL.

Mr. BELL. Mr. Speaker, during the latter part of October, 1896, while crossing the plains of Nebraska, I glanced at a morning paper. My eyes immediately fastened upon a familiar picture, with an inscription below, "Ex-Speaker CRISP is dead!" That sad announcement was followed by the crowding upon me of the many reasons he had for coveting a long life. I was forcibly reminded that nature had generously given him a comely and commanding presence; that his nature had been formed into such a happy blending of sunshine, good-fellowship, and frank hospitality that his society was greatly sought, and life should have been to him an unbroken pleasure; that through his many commendable attributes he had become preeminently the favored son of his own great State, and was in sight of the goal of his political ambition—the United States Senate—when death overtook him and ended earthly ambition. But sad as these misfortunes are for him and his immediate friends, the calamity is infinitely more deplorable as a great public loss.

The death of an individual rarely disturbs the general current of the orderly course of human action, but occasionally one does fall by the wayside who leaves such a void as is difficult to fill. Such a one we lament to-day. His mental alignment approximated perfect equilibrium. No one faculty had been dwarfed to give a surplus to others. Therefore he never startled the world with any phenomenal outburst of genius, nor did he ever disappoint his friends by descending to mediocrity. He was of the solid, even-tempered, well-balanced order of men to whom only can the safety and perpetuity of a great country be confidently intrusted.

It is true he was imbued with a laudable ambition to serve his countrymen in public places, not for pecuniary compensation, as mercenary aspirations were beneath his high standard. He was not ambitious that he might revel in the glare of official society, as such were too empty and sterile for his strong common-sense view of the real pleasures and amenities of human life. He sought to serve his fellows because they evinced a desire for his services and because he believed that he could serve them well, and he believed that his policies enacted into law would inure to the greatest good to the greatest and most deserving number.

The Populist party in Congress, for whom I speak as well as for myself, has every reason to pay high tribute to his memory. While Speaker, we were few in number, misunderstood, and grossly misrepresented by politicians and the partisan press, often intentionally, and more frequently through ignorance of our intentions and aspirations; but he was too large to be tainted with bigotry or intolerance, the worst enemies of mankind. He never wavered a hair's breadth in doing us complete justice at all times. We never visited him at his private apartments that his easy geniality and open hospitality did not convince us that he fully recognized that he was Speaker of the whole House. We never approached him in the Speaker's chair that the hand of good-fellowship and some friendly verbal greeting was not extended. He never denied our petitions without giving such cogent reasons therefor and in so becoming a manner that we acquiesced in the conclusion that he could not be expected to do less.

He granted our applications in such an unostentatious manner that we were sent away feeling that a right and not a favor had been granted.

He possessed none of the elements of the bigot—never fastened any doors between him and the public. He preferred to be with and of the people. None knew better than he the danger of tyrannical majorities visiting oppression and injustice on struggling minorities. He was never a representative of any special class or section of the country. He was a statesman of the highest and purest type, and a representative of the whole people of the whole country. In this matchless contest for the supremacy of the people the loss of such a representative, so pure a type of the founders of this Government, is indeed a great public calamity. When I returned to Washington and met the colored boy who used to care for his room, with moistened eyes, he said, "We have sustained a great loss since you went away in the death of Speaker CRISP," and added, "Everything that knew that man loved him."

That is greater eulogy than I am capable of pronouncing. After all is said and done, the real character of a man is most truly photographed and known in his home life and by those who serve him.

ADDRESS OF MR. WHEELER

Mr. WHEELER. Mr. Speaker, when the Angel of Death received the spirit of CHARLES FREDERICK CRISP, a man was taken from this world who had won the love of his State, the confidence and admiration of the entire South, and the respect of our whole country. As a native Georgian, I take special pride in the great distinction achieved by him whose death we mourn.

Mr. CRISP always performed every duty in a most creditable manner. When little more than a boy, he was a brave soldier and officer in the Army of Northern Virginia, following the sword of Robert E. Lee in the many battles fought by that illustrious commander. With the return of peace he retired to his home and became a lawyer, respected for his ability, learning, and fidelity. As solicitor-general of his district and as judge of one of the superior courts of Georgia, he earned the highest commendations.

He was twice elected to preside over the popular branch of the Congress of the United States, and during a service of fourteen years in this body he certainly reached a most exalted place among the statesmen of America. His reputation as a parliamentarian and a just presiding officer had extended throughout the civilized world.

While in the midst of the performance of these high duties, he was appointed and urged by the governor of Georgia to accept a seat in the Senate of the United States, but his high conception of the duty he owed to those who had elected him to preside over this body constrained him to decline the proffered honor; but the people of Georgia, appreciating his noble character and superb qualities, seized the first opportunity after the expiration of his term as Speaker to do him honor, and with almost unprecedented unanimity elected him to the office which but a short time before he had felt it his duty to decline—the highest office in their gift—one which he was qualified in an eminent degree to adorn; but just as the decree of the people was to be recorded, it was met by the dread messenger, Death.

Well may it be said of him, right worthily he fought life's battle and won his way to fame; and the people who loved to honor him in life will revere and cherish his memory in death, and his name will be arrayed among those illustrious statesmen of Georgia who did their full part in perfecting the system of government which has built up this great and prosperous Republic.

In the midst of his strength and usefulness, before age had made slow his footstep, or chilled the warmth of his heart, or dimmed the brightness of his eye, or withered the brilliancy of the intellect which had served his country and his State so long and so well, surrounded by the shadows and hills and sunshine of his own beloved Georgia, in the midst of his countrymen and the beloved family which knew his greatness best of all, he fought his last battle with sickness and pain, and answered to the roll call of the Great Captain, and passed from the mystery of this life upon earth into that greater life "whose portals we call death," though there can be no death to those who leave their names enshrined in the hearts of their countrymen.

In our journey of life, in the Halls of Congress, in his old accustomed place, in the sunny vales of his home in the far Southland, we shall greet CHARLES FREDERICK CRISP no more.   He has met his "Pilot face to face," and has crossed over the river and is at "rest under the shade of the trees."

I can but echo the words of one who knew him well: "Over his dreaming face, in the shadow of the Georgia hills, we say good night to him, but good morning to his enduring fame."

ADDRESS OF MR. WOODARD.

Mr. WOODARD. Mr. Speaker, it is a loving service to those who knew, valued, and honored him, to speak in memory of the life and character of CHARLES FREDERICK CRISP.

As a private soldier, he was brave and faithful; as judge of the superior court, he shed luster upon the judiciary of his State; as a member of Congress, he was long the trusted leader of his party; as Speaker, he was a master of parliamentary procedure, a model presiding officer, firm and resolute, but always courteous; with an attractive personality, indomitable courage, great prudence, an earnest partisan because he believed the policies of his party, if enacted into laws, would redound to the honor and welfare of his country; a statesman in its best and broadest sense, his party and his country have sustained a great loss in his untimely death.

I do not propose, Mr. Speaker, to review in detail the early history or services of Mr. CRISP. That has been done by others who have known him longer, and who have in appropriate and eloquent words portrayed his exalted worth as a citizen, his valuable services to his party and country.

I first met him at the beginning of the Fifty-third Congress, when I entered upon my service as a member of this House, and my admiration for his character as a man and as a statesman increased with the passing years.

When but a boy, only 16 years of age, animated by that patriotic spirit which followed him through life, we find him a volunteer soldier in the Confederate Army, where he served until the end of the war. Immediately after its close he commenced the study of law, and in a few years attained a high rank in his chosen profession. He was elected solicitor-general and judge of the superior court, and while on the bench was elected to Congress. He had served in the House but a short time when his conspicuous ability pointed him out, as if by intuition, as the leader of his party on the floor. Having been assigned by common consent to that honorable and responsible position, it was manifest that he was a born leader, equal to every emergency, always ready, always wise, always able, and ever true to his convictions of duty. While possessed of that firmness and true courage so necessary to constitute a successful leader, Mr. CRISP was withal a modest gentleman, and never forgot the amenities and courtesies due his opponents. On all occasions he exhibited those manly and gentle virtues which never fail to win our warmest admiration and tenderest regard.

In the Fifty-second and Fifty-third Congresses he was elected Speaker of this House, and in that delicate and responsible position he more than sustained his justly earned reputation for ability, firmness, fairness, and courtesy. His record as presiding officer will compare favorably with that of the most distinguished parliamentarians who preceded him. In every position he was called upon to fill, Mr. CRISP measured up to the fullest expectations of his friends, and his whole life affords a bright example for the young men of our country to emulate.

As a soldier, as a citizen, as a judge, as a member of Congress, as Speaker, as the great leader of a great party, he was ever faithful to himself, to his people, to his party, to his country, and to his Maker. Those high, noble, and sincere virtues which made Mr. CRISP a conspicuous leader in American politics and constituted him a pure and unsullied statesman were a part of his nature, and they appear with equal beauty and brightness in his private character. In all the private and social relations of life the same purity of character, honesty of purpose, and noble aspirations which distinguished his public life made him a model citizen, a true and constant friend, a loving and tender husband, an affectionate father, and a Christian gentleman.

It was my fortune, Mr. Speaker, to be constantly associated with him during the last four years, as we boarded at the same hotel in this city. The more I saw of him the more I appreciated his high qualities and the beauties and virtues of his private life. During the latter part of the first session of this Congress the health of Mr. CRISP became impaired, but his friends hoped his suffering would be only temporary. After adjournment he sought relief in the pure and invigorating climate of western North Carolina; but the disease which had attacked him was a fatal malady, and his indomitable will and brave heart struggled in vain against the inevitable result. Death came to him in the very zenith of his career. It came to him when his party and country seemed to be in special need of his wise counsel and safe leadership. It came when he was so soon to receive at the hands of a grateful people the high office which had been the ambition of his life. Why should he have been taken at this time? We would not question God's providences, so mysterious in so many ways. Beautifully has it been said by another:

There is an existence beyond the present life where all shall be made clear. We shall see as we are seen ; we shall know even as we are known. Mr. Dickens made the poor, idiotic Barnaby and the coarse, strong Hugh, of the Maypole Inn, hold conversation about the visible wonders of the heavens, and they inquire of each other whence comes the light of the innumerable stars that dot the skies. When they were both under sentence of death, and just before the dawn of day were led across the prison yard toward the place of execution, Barnaby, looking upward toward the myriad lights of the night, exclaims: "Hugh, we shall know what makes the stars shine now."

Our faith here to-day ought to exceed that of the poor simpleton created by the imagination of the novelist. Not only shall we know what makes the stars shine, but all the wonders of the vast universe shall be open to our search. Our homes shall be among the heavens; the problems that our burdened souls have studied so despairingly shall be happily solved, and we may even become participators in the knowledge and power of Him—

> Whose power o'er moving worlds presides,
> Whose voice created and whose wisdom guides.

To this felicity the friend we now with tenderness remember has already fully advanced. We would not, if we could, bring him back to earth, slowly and painfully to die again. We wait, reverently and hopefully, for the summons to us to join him in some star that is shining, from eternity to eternity, with unfading luster in God's illimitable wilderness of worlds.

ADDRESS OF MR. LAYTON.

Mr. LAYTON. Mr. Speaker, what is an ideal man? Who is a perfect man? Who can fully describe him? Where can he be found? These questions present a fruitful and varied field for the writer and speaker, so broad and varied in fact that I do not deem it wise or appropriate to enter thereon or therein save only for the purpose of making a few observations this afternoon more or less pertinent to the occasion.

Hence I would inquire, What is your ideal of an American statesman? Where say you he can be found? How would you describe him to your hearers? Have you ever seen his counterpart? Is he now living or dead? Should these inquiries be addressed to myself, I would be constrained to answer in substance: I have never yet seen in its entirety my ideal of an American statesman; neither do I know where he can be found, nor can I fully or satisfactorily describe him to you. Yet I well remember one who came so near to my ideal that I do not now hesitate to accept him as such; but with a sadness I can but illy express, I would say he is no longer living.

Perhaps my ideal is too exalted. Perhaps in fact he never existed, can not, nor ever will. If so, I much regret it, for as I now view it in the light of more or less intercourse and association with many of our American statesmen, during the last six years especially, I do not regard my ideal as unreasonable or impossible of attainment. And as an American citizen who loves and admires her men and her institutions and believes in her continuing progress and advancement, it affords me great pleasure to say that, while none of her statesmen of my acquaintance come up to the exact mark or line, yet many come so near it that I shall ever refer to the fact with pride and satisfaction. So near have so many come to this exacting ideal that I can have no fear for the future growth and welfare of our now great Republic under their continuing care and guidance.

In my humble judgment, an ideal, a real American statesman, in these times especially, when aristocracy and plutocracy are so freely referred to and censured, should at all times be purely democratic in his ways, manner, and conduct with all his fellow-men, and yet always dignified. He should of course, be educated, able, and intellectual. He should never be a demagogue. He should be affable and pleasant and still dignified. He should be firm and decisive, yet considerate and forbearing, especially with his inferiors in intellect and experience. He should not be sarcastic to individuals, no matter how caustic he may be in his references to criticism of classes or parties, and above and beyond all, unselfishness and patriotism should guide and control his every public utterance and action. We doubtless have had in the past and now have many American statesmen who fulfill most of these requirements, if not quite all. I can pay no higher or more just tribute to the memory of CHARLES FREDERICK CRISP than to say that, taking him all in all, he came nearer doing so than any other with whom I have ever had the honor of an acquaintanceship. None who knew him well will resent this statement or take offense thereat. He was always manly and dignified in his manner and conduct, yet ever affable and pleasant, whether on the floor of this House, in the committee room, in the Speaker's chair, on the street, in public

gatherings, or in his own household.   He was always positive and firm in his convictions and opinions, and yet ever
kind and considerate with those who might differ with him.
In all matters he was totally unselfish, and true patriotism—
the general welfare of his country—seemed to guide him in
all his official conduct.   He was not a great orator, but was
a great, concise debater.   As a husband and father, he
was ever loving, kind, and gentle.   Those who knew him
best appreciated him the most.

Term after term the people of his Congressional district
returned him to Congress with an almost unanimous voice.
In the Fifty-second Congress, when his party came in power,
he was elected to the high and important office of Speaker
of this House—the most important position in the Union
next to that of President.   The Firty-third Congress again
so honored him without any opposition from his own party.
He administered the office with great ability and impartiality.   At the beginning of the present Congress he was
honored by his party associates as their choice for the same
position.   While serving in this exalted position the governor of his State, in willing obedience to the wishes of the
people, tendered him the Senatorship by appointment to fill
a vacancy in the United States Senate.   And yet, while
desiring the position thus so kindly offered him, he promptly
declined the appointment on the sole and patriotic ground
that he could serve his country and party the better by
retaining the Speakership.   Soon afterwards he was duly
recommended as a candidate for the United States Senate
by his party in Georgia with substantial unanimity.   But,
alas, before he could take his seat therein, ruthless Death
cut him down.   But recently his young but worthy son,
Charles R. Crisp, was elected a member of this House

without opposition to succeed his illustrious father and fill out his unexpired term in this Congress. On the first day of this session Mr. CRISP's untimely death was acknowledged by an appropriate resolution, followed by immediate adjournment for the day in honor of his memory. All, regardless of section or party, conceded that his premature death in the prime of his manhood was a great loss to his State and the nation. No man, no newspaper, said an unkind word of him, but all, as we are now doing, sincerely regret and mourn his loss. Indeed may we say:

> None knew him but to love him,
> None named him but to praise.

Ohio mourns with Georgia over the loss of her distinguished son.

To every American citizen who desires or intends to follow public official life I most sincerely commend the life, character, and history of Mr. CRISP. May we, our children, and our children's children ever emulate his noble example.

ADDRESS OF MR. BANKHEAD.

Mr. BANKHEAD. Mr. Speaker, to-day we stop for a brief season the onward current of our everyday duties to pay tribute to one who in life was most himself when engaged, as we are daily engaged, in the business and affairs of this House. In the death of CHARLES FREDERICK CRISP, representative life in America lost one of its most brilliant ornaments and our nation one of its purest and most exalted statesmen.

Standing now in this presence, about to speak my words of tribute to our dead friend and associate, I feel crowding on me emotions of peculiar sadness. All the keen pain and anguish that touched my heart at the immediate occasion of his death are renewed, and what I would say is almost stayed. In our greetings and farewells we have no set and studied phrases. When we grasp the hand of one we may not have seen for years, or come to part with one we may never see again, then it is that speech is hollow and but sound, and the beaming eyes, the quivering lips, the whole face give expression to an emotion beyond the reach of words.

Sir, when Mr. CRISP died, he had barely passed the half-century mark. Born in the year 1845, educated in the common schools of his State, a mere lad of 16 he entered the Confederate Army. From his enlistment in May, 1861, to his capture in May, 1864, he was a brave soldier, winning the confidence and love of his superiors. He knew the true import of the word duty, and all his subsequent career shows the influence on his life of the rigorous discipline of active warfare. Of the part he took in this mighty conflict I know how he felt, and that feeling I find embodied in the tribute paid by the distinguished Senator from Ohio [Mr. Sherman] on the late Senator Randall Lee Gibson, of Louisiana:

We have come to regard this fierce and sanguinary struggle as an inheritance from our fathers, growing out of an honest difference of opinion as to the framework of our Government. Poor human nature could provide no arbitrator to settle this contention, but now that it has been settled by a sacrifice of life and treasure almost unexampled in human history, it can be truly said that the result is heartily acquiesced in, and that no slumbering fires can rise from the ashes of the civil war to disturb the unity, integrity, and power of this great Republic.

One year after the close of hostilities found him admitted to the bar and located at Ellaville, Ga., in the practice of the law, called by Burke " one of the first and noblest of human sciences." For six years he toiled at his profession, struggling as its younger members do with an effort to build up a paying practice. However, in 1872 his success had won him the first of the series of offices which was to end by his being the choice of the Empire State of the South for Senator in the United States Congress. In this year he was appointed solicitor-general of the southwestern judicial circuit, and after a twelvemonth he was reappointed for four years. In 1873 he removed to Americus, where he spent the remainder of his life. From 1877 to 1882 he was one of the superior court judges. The latter year closed his professional work as an active practitioner. These sixteen years of his life represent a career full of interest. He was a successful lawyer. His ability commanded his first office and enabled him to hold it. As an advocate he was earnest and fearless. Transferred to the bench, his facilities easily adjusted themselves to the severe exactions of the position, and he was all that is looked for in the term an "upright and a just judge."

Taking his seat in the Forty-eighth Congress, he early assumed that prominent place and developed those splendid qualities of leadership which won for him the Speaker's chair of the Fifty-second and Fifty-third Congresses. His life and work here are known and read of all men. I know that I am in the limits of exact statement when I say that there are no acts of his while in this body that will not stand the test of the most searching criticism. In his relations with his fellow-members he was always genial and pleasant. He seemed always happy; and while he might be leading a galloping charge on this floor, his natural manner never became offensive, and at its conclusion his perennial humor and serene temper returned. In his work as a Representative he was always busy, and no duty did he leave unperformed if possible of attention. His constituents had unbounded confidence and trust in him and in his power to serve them.

Perhaps it was in his course as Speaker in this body that he displayed qualities of a higher order than in any other field. His ability as a parliamentarian was remarkable. In his incumbency of this exalted seat and in his administration of its duties he won the admiration of his political opponents and was the idol of his friends. He was essentially fair and just. It was his desire to do right, and this he did at all times, as he conceived it. Quick, decisive, impartial, unfailing in resource, he must be ranked with his greatest predecessors.

While he was a good soldier, a successful lawyer, a learned judge, and a leader in the greatest representative assembly in the world, it is as a Christian gentleman he must be accorded the greatest honor. In his home life, which I can not here invade, he was the devoted, tender, and loving husband, and the ever fond, indulgent parent. I was first attracted to him because of his orderly habits of life and his loyal love of his home.   Day by day I saw him come and go, in the Halls of Congress, in his intercourse with the world, in the bosom of his family, and I saw in his life the well-nigh perfect man.

But he is gone from us now.   In a little while we should have seen him take his seat in the other end of the Capitol, but instead he has gone up higher, "to where, beyond these voices, there is peace."   The journey done, he is resting now; he is sleeping the sleep that knows no waking, careless alike of the day dawn or the twilight.   For him the dark night of death was the sunburst of an eternal hereafter.

> I will not say, God's ordinance
>   Of death is blown in every wind,
> For that is not a common chance
>   That takes away a noble mind.
>
> His memory long will live alone
>   In all our hearts, as mournful light
> That broods above the fallen sun
>   And dwells in heaven half the night.

ADDRESS OF MR. McLAURIN.

Mr. McLaurin. Mr. Speaker, no man can foretell the mysterious issues of life and death.   Few who saw CHARLES FREDERICK CRISP at the close of the last session thought that death would so soon cast its pale shadow upon that apparently robust body and vigorous mind.

How uncertain is the future! To-day life is bright, the sea is calm, the tide swells high and strong.   To-morrow the tide turns; business trouble, sickness, or death robs us of hope and pleasure.   From the calm and beautiful harbor where we floated so confidently we are rudely tossed out upon the wide ocean.   The horizon stretches far beyond our vision, and the heave of its restless waves comes from depths that are unfathomable.   Vainly struggling, we either sink to the tranquil depths, where all is peace, or, tempest-torn and faint, are cast upon the shore.   Well may the poet exclaim:

> What is life? A brief delight;
> A sun, scarce brightening ere it sink in night;
> A flower, at morning fresh, at noon decayed;
> A still, swift river, gliding into shade.

The man who would know its true secret must learn to live "in deeds, not years; in thoughts, not breaths; in feelings, not in figures on a dial"—to count time in heart throbs.   He most lives who thinks most, feels noblest, acts best.

I think Mr. CRISP grasped the true meaning of life and lived "in deeds, not years; thoughts, not breaths."

The first time I saw him, the thing that struck me most forcibly was the strong, cheerful, and kindly expression of his face.   He had a hearty, genial manner, with a pleasant

smile and kind word for everyone. I can well believe
that in the home circle he was gentle, tender, and considerate; his sunny nature must have gladdened the hearts
and lives of those who were traveling the journey with
him. It is, however, for those more intimate to speak of
him in private life. As a colleague from a sister State, it is
simply my wish to pay a brief but sincere tribute to him as
a public man. Those who differed with him politically
will testify that, while firm in his convictions, he was generous and tolerant of the opinion of others, while those of
us who accepted his leadership will say that, like Joseph
of Arimathea, "He was a just man and good counsellor."

For the great, patient, toiling masses he had an active and
sincere sympathy. He never lost sight of the fact that he
was a public servant, sent here to represent the will of the
majority. He was an ideal Representative, never imagining
himself wiser than the collective thought of the people who
sent him here. He was in close touch with his people, with
a thorough knowledge of their sentiments upon all public
questions; and, after all, true statesmanship in a representative government simply means the needs and wishes of the
people translated into law. The people love and appreciate
a faithful representative. What a graceful and touching
compliment they paid Mr. Crisp.

When death came, they sent his son to occupy his vacant
chair in this House. Indeed, there was no more beautiful
sight than the almost brotherly confidence and intimacy that
seemed to exist between this father and son, and the people
of Georgia honored themselves in paying such a tribute to
the memory of their dead. I am sure that the mantle fell
upon worthy shoulders, and that the trust will be regarded
sacred by his successor and namesake.

It was while engaged in a canvass of his State for the Senatorship that the premonitory symptoms were felt of that disease which ended his life. Although apparently sound and vigorous, he probably had full knowledge of this vital weakness, but he did not allow it to deter him from his work. I met him day after day in the committee room, cheerful and confident, while he was always at his post on the floor of the House, prompt and vigilant. It may literally be said that "he died in the harness." We are told that when that knight of old, without fear or reproach, Chevalier Bayard, was wounded unto death, he commanded his attendants to prop him up against a tree with his face to the enemy; he then, after taking the sacrament, died with this beautiful sentiment on his lips: "The justice of Almighty God will be tempered by the blood of our Lord Jesus Christ." With a character as pure and spotless, with a courage as chivalrous, and a like trust in the justice and mercy of the same God, died, without fear or reproach, this gallant knight of a modern day.

The State of Georgia, Mr. Speaker, has been prolific in great men. At the mention of her name the mind reverts to Alexander H. Stephens, the conservative and sagacious statesman; to Ben Hill, the eloquent and gifted orator; to the lion-like and majestic Toombs, with his fiery and irresistible logic; but, sir, great as are these, Mr. CRISP is well worthy a place in their ranks. The times did not afford him the same opportunity to display the most striking qualities of statesmanship that they did Stephens, and history may not accord him as high rank; in the realms of oratory he was not, perhaps, the equal of Toombs or Hill, but as an allround man—statesman, orator, and debater— he was the peer of Georgia's greatest. Of great practical common sense, modest, imperturbable, evenly poised, and cool, it was impossible to throw him off his balance.

As the representative of a powerful majority, wielding the Speaker's gavel, he was impartial, courteous, and kind; as the leader of the minority, he was cautious, tactful, and ready of resource, and it seemed to me that his masterly qualities were never better displayed than in the latter rôle. He had a clear, clean-cut, incisive style, with an entire absence of attempt at display. In a calm, sensible, business-like manner, he went right to the marrow of a question.

He inspired confidence, and men trusted Mr. CRISP and accepted his leadership because they knew that he would never say or do a foolish thing nor be caught in an untenable position. Preeminently a safe man, it could be confidently counted upon that he would say the right thing at the right time and do the right thing in the right place. Fully developed mentally, physically, and morally, he was ready for and equal to every emergency. No one in this House ever saw him on any occasion, however difficult, when he did not meet the requirements in every respect. He saw in an instant a weakness in the position of an adversary, and his thorough knowledge of parliamentary usage enabled him to seize every advantage. Under the most trying circumstances he fully met and often exceeded the expectation of his friends.

Mr. Speaker, it is in such an hour as this, when the great and powerful are cut short in the midst of their career, that we are most forcibly reminded of our weakness and dependence upon God. Death is the great leveler; he makes no distinction between prince and pauper. It is the same everywhere; in the humble cot or the bright palace, in the wild forest or the brilliant city, in the swamps or upon the mountain top, to the humble laborer or the great statesman, the same dread summons chills the blood and freezes the heart. Christ, and Christ alone, can dispel the pall of gloomy terror that hovers about the bed of death. The genius of man and the wisdom of the ages offer no other solution. The "Go in peace" and "Thy sins are forgiven thee" must be spoken to each, and is our safe retreat.

It is not given to many to rise to the elevated position occupied by Mr. CRISP. All can not be eagles, but each of us has his work, great or small; and we are taught that the manner in which it is performed is of more account than the magnitude of the task accomplished. If the trend of our life is for good, if its course is ever upward and onward, if its thought and inspiration are in harmony with the purpose of Providence in creating us, however insignificant our work may appear to others, surely we shall find in the great final day of account that we have not lived and toiled in vain.

As members of this House we lead here busy, active lives, and when we are at home the turmoil, strife, and jealousies of political rivalry leave little time to prepare for the "great beyond." It is well, therefore, on occasions of this character to pause a moment and draw home the solemn lesson each for himself.

Let us not be unmindful of the fact that a great leader, one of the busiest in our number, yet found time to seek that peace which will sustain the faltering soul in that last dark hour and make it radiant with the never-dying hope of eternal life. Mr. CRISP was a consistent and faithful member of the Methodist Church. After all the triumphs which crowned a brilliant and successful career, I doubt not that if to-day his well-known voice could be heard in this Chamber he would reecho the dying words of the founder of his Church, John Wesley, "Best of all, the Lord is with us."

ADDRESS OF MR. MCCREARY.

Mr. McCreary. Mr. Speaker, there is no arena which death does not invade. There is no place too sacred for its touch. There is nothing living on earth, no matter how great or small, how pure or vile, how rich or poor, but must finally succumb to the dread destroyer. There is always somewhere—

> Some heart that is bleeding,
> Some eye that is weeping,
> Some home that is draped,
> Some loved person dead.

When our comrade dies, when our coworker is stricken down full of hope and high purposes and great achievements, when he who has helped to make history and participated with us in the important legislation of our country is taken away in the prime and vigor of a splendid manhood, when his ability, integrity, and devotion to the public weal are most appreciated and most needed, we realize fully that death is very near to us, and that our affliction is severe, and our country's loss is great.

Others have given detailed accounts of the life and career of Charles Frederick Crisp. I shall speak mainly of his character and his services in the legislative forum, where I knew him best and where I respected and admired him as a leader and loved him as a friend.

I first met him when I commenced my service as a Representative in Congress in 1885. My admiration for him grew as I became better acquainted with him, and I was deeply impressed with his genial, pleasant nature, and with the promptness and readiness with which he met every emergency.

I regarded him as a noble type of American manhood, able, logical, self-made, and self-reliant, and always courteous, courageous, and true.

He was firm and sincere in his convictions, faithful to his friends, liberal to his opponents, fair, just, and conscientious, and unceasing in the discharge of his duties as a Representative.

He was the faithful friend and champion of the people. He loved liberty, civil, political, and religious, and he was devoted to popular government.

He was both a patriot and a philanthropist. No man gave greater and more continued evidence of his love of country, and no man was more prompt to aid a friend or give freely to the needy and deserving.

He worked for what he regarded as the rights of the people, and did all in his power to protect the interests and promote the welfare and prosperity of the Republic, and the radiance of his integrity and the brightness of his honor were never assailed or questioned.

He was devoted to his wife, his children, and his home, and no husband or father was ever the recipient of more love and respect. His family circle was full of affection and sweet communion, and here he illustrated how happy a man could be who was trying to do his duty to his God, his family, and his country.

His life and achievements illustrated not only the splendid opportunities of our great Republic, but showed also the honorable success and great renown that will crown earnest efforts, strict integrity, and steadfast devotion to duty.

The first and last conspicuous events in his life showed not only his courage, ability, and self-reliance, but also the confidence, admiration, and love lavished upon him by those who knew him best. At 16 years of age he proved his courage and self-reliance by enlisting as a soldier in the Confederate Army and bravely fighting until the close of the war for what he believed to be right. When he was 51 years of age, the people of Georgia, who had for more than a quarter of a century studied his public service and his fidelity to his State and nation, sought to confer upon him the highest honor in their gift by making him a United States Senator, and practically all of the State senators and representatives elected were instructed by the people to honor him with this great office; but his death prevented this great trust and well-merited distinction from being conferred upon him.

His views on finance, taxation, education, commerce, agriculture, an economical administration of the Government, the sovereignty of the people, and the independence of the coordinate departments of the Government, and on all other important questions presented, were often announced in strong and eloquent speeches, which are found in nearly every volume of the Congressional Record issued since his service as Representative commenced.

As an earnest, fearless champion of Democracy, he was always ready to defend his party and his principles, and he loved to uphold and support the teachings and doctrines of Jefferson and Jackson.

It was as Speaker of the House of Representatives he gained his highest honors and made himself most conspicuous before the country. His knowledge of parliamentary law and procedure, his equipoise, and the ease, dignity, firmness, and fairness with which he presided made him popular with the members of all political parties and enabled him to conduct the business with order and dispatch.

I believe the dispassionate judgment of those over whom he presided for four years is that he is entitled to be remembered as one of the ablest and most accomplished of the Speakers of the House of Representatives.

The history of Georgia is luminous with the names of brilliant, earnest, and faithful statesmen. Among the ablest and strongest of that great galaxy the name of Mr. CRISP has taken its permanent place. His fame does not belong to Georgia alone nor to the South, but to the whole Republic, and in Kentucky we will cherish his memory, and his fame will survive along with that of the other dead statesmen, jurists, and heroes—Hill, Toombs, Colquitt, and Brown—who did so much to make Georgia conspicuous and illustrious.

It is written in one of the tender and beautiful legends which the Talmud has preserved that at the moment of the death of a good man memories of his love and charity and good deeds float through his mind to cheer and console him as his spirit soars away from the cares and conflicts, the joys and sorrows, of life. If this be true, our friend in his last moments, when the darkness of death was settling upon him and the first glimpse of immortality was beginning to be seen, had much to soothe and comfort him. Reviewing his life, his early manhood, his mature years, he could see glittering and glistening along his way good deeds which benefited his fellow-men in the State and in the nation. He could see fidelity and devotion to loved ones at home; he could see charity and love, fragrant as flowers in spring-time, beautifying and chastening a life well spent in the service of his God and his country, and at the end of it all I believe he could hear the welcome plaudit, "Well done, thou good and faithful servant; enter thou into the joy of thy Lord."

ADDRESS OF MR. WELLINGTON.

Mr. WELLINGTON. Mr. Speaker, amid the lengthening shadows of this midwinter afternoon the Representatives of our nation have met to mourn the untimely ending of a great career. The strong voice of active legislation is at rest, the fierce contention of partisan debate is hushed, and in their stead solemn decorum and order reign. To-day we are concerned not with the living, in the present or the future, but the dead and the past. We call a halt in the march of life; we turn from the busy scenes and activities of living men to the grave that nestles with many others in distant Georgia, in that place set apart for the habitations of the dead; and, as we stand before it with sad and sorrowful mien, I would lay a simple flower there while others may place a wreath of amaranth upon it as a tribute to the memory of CHARLES FREDERICK CRISP.

From the quiet portals of the grave there come none but "fond regrets and tender recollections." Resentments are forgotten, faults forgiven, and remembrance portrays to us in vivid pictures the virtues and noble actions of the departed.

As we unroll the canvas of the last half century, whereon time hath painted in ineffaceable colors the life history of the distinguished man whom we mourn, there are few foibles to condone and much that was noble to commend.

The annals of a nation are written in the biography of its great men. The mass of the people have no history. The record of their lives is short and simple, and remains ever the same. They are born, they live, they die, and are forgotten; generation after generation meets the same fate.

We blunder through youth, struggle in manhood; and if perchance we are fortunate enough to reach old age, it is a scene of vain and unavailing regrets. But there are men who, by the force and power of talent or genius, indomitable will, or never-ceasing perseverance, lift themselves above their fellows, and in the record of their lives write history for their people. Such a man was Mr. CRISP. Not a brilliant man, perhaps; not one whose name will flash with lustrous light, for he did not live in a time when splendid effulgence reigned. Yet when the records of this commonplace period of American national life are made up, his figure will stand out in bold relief as one who stood by his section, who partook of the bitterness of sectional strife, and yet was broad enough to rise above rancor, and developed into a national character, which, though tinged with sectionalism, grew gradually until he reached the loftier elements of patriotism, humanity, and a gentleness rarely observed among men.

Born in the stormy times when the unavoidable conflict was rapidly approaching, he had reached the days of youth when sectional strife began. The bitter struggles of that eventful period have become a story of the past, and a generation of men have been born and grown into manhood since the great civil war. To me it is a memory of childhood. Yet I can well remember when the two opinions of government, which had existed antagonistic to each other since the formation of the Republic, divided our land and arrayed one part against the other.

In the North there had grown the idea of a strong Federal Government, such as had been portrayed by the Declaration of Independence. In the South there was the sentiment of a Confederation of States, such as had been contemplated in the Articles of Federation which bound the Colonies in the Revolutionary war. These two rival principles met upon the border; there sentiment was divided, and therefore upon the borderland can be found that judgment which perhaps will give in more impartial manner credit to each and both for the valor, heroism, and self-sacrifice with which each section maintained what it believed to be right.

When the great struggle came, Mr. CRISP, who was then a youth, cast his fortunes with his native State. Georgia had broken the bonds that bound her to the Federal Union. She had joined herself to that other government which had been named by the Southern States. Mr. CRISP had been reared in the school of State rights, of sovereignty for the Commonwealth, and therefore it was but natural to him to give allegiance to the Commonwealth which, though not the place of his birth, had given him sustenance through childhood and youth, and from which he had received all she had to give.

Amid all the changeful fortunes and vicissitudes of internecine strife the days of his youth passed into manhood, and in the fortunes of war he became a prisoner in the hands of the Federal troops. There he remained until the conflict was ended and the great question upon which the perpetuity of this Government depended was forever put at rest. The first period of his life was closed. The sentiment of State sovereignty, which had colored his youth and led him to take up arms at the behest of his State against the General Government, was dead—aye, more ; buried beneath four years of weary marching, attacks and repulses, victories and defeats, a million lives, and billions of treasure. It was a lesson in national life which every nation must learn, and which, thanks be to God, the American nation has successfully committed to memory. It made a deep impression upon Mr. CRISP's life; it fashioned all the years that were to come, and converted much of the partisan into a judicial temperament. He began life on his own account, studied law, and entered into its practice. Success attended his efforts, judicial honors were given him, and then there came into his life another ambition, which led him into the path where he was most needed. The bitter passions and intense prejudices of sectional strife do not pass away in the fading of a moon nor yet in the circling of the seasons of one short year. They die gradually, and the people who would throw them off need the calm judgment, the sober second thought of men who can lead them conservatively, who will appeal to nobler sentiments and broader views, and no man in the past two decades has rendered greater service to his common country in this direction than Mr. CRISP. His whole course in the House of Representatives, while it manifested the fact that he was true to the atmosphere in which he lived and faithful to the people whom he served, demonstrated that he could look beyond the narrow confines of his State, view the broad expanse of our country, and, step by step, guide the Southern States to the common vantage ground where hands should be clasped and common cause made for the whole American people.

When I met him first, but little over a year ago, I knew him only by the reputation he had made as the leader of the political organization to which he belonged; knew him by the record he had made as Speaker of the House of Representatives. I esteemed him, admired him, honored him, and personal contact but intensified that sentiment and feeling.

As a leader of men of his own opinion, he was neither rude nor masterful. To the opposition he was very fair, just, and frequently charitable. To tyros and beginners he

was not only gentle, but generous, and he had about him
the subtle quality of standing firm upon his own ground,
yet winning the confidence, trust, and good graces of his
adversaries.

I saw him last upon the floor of this House, when insid-
ious disease had begun its work, but he bore it bravely, and
by strength of will and nerve attempted to win the terrible
battle of life against death.   Even then the silent angel
poised the dread shaft which ere long was to speed and
strike him down.   The flowers of spring had bloomed and
faded when he departed for his home, there to engage in
the contest which was to bring him further honors from
the people of his State.   Summer passed, the harvests of
autumn were gathered, and the winds of approaching winter were beginning to sigh and moan among the trees when
the final summons came, and the wires flashed to friend and
foe the news that saddened one and all, giving the tidings
of his death.

The record of his life is made up.   It is fair and beautiful; and the characteristic which shall make him loved most
among our people is that he was just and generous toward
all, and mingled with justice and generosity that love which
is the best part of all men, for, in the language of the
Ancient Mariner—

> He prayeth well who loveth well
> Both man and bird and beast;
> He prayeth best who loveth best
> All things both great and small;
> For the dear God who loveth us,
> He made and loveth all.

Thus we may leave him, life's faithful mission accomplished and the enigma of the hereafter solved.   His memory may be safely intrusted to the people with whom he
lived and who now dwell where his ashes rest.

ADDRESS OF MR. TATE.

Mr. TATE. Mr. Speaker, we pause amidst the stormy strife of life's fierce battles and the busy, bustling scenes of party contention and international disturbance to pay trib- ute to the memory, recall the services, tell of the exalted character, and recount the many virtues of one who has left his impress upon the age in which he lived. A great leader has fallen. When the future historian comes to record the names of the illustrious statesmen who have been the pride and glory of our common country, that of CHARLES FREDERICK CRISP will shine forth among the first and the foremost and shed luster upon the greatest and the best.

When Attorney-General Cushing, on December 9, 1853, announced to the Supreme Court the death of that great and good man William R. King, Vice-President of the United States, he said, among other beautiful things con- cerning the dead statesman, these grand words, which are so appropriate to this occasion that I take the liberty of transcribing them:

He stands to the memory in sharp outline, as it were, against the sky like some chiseled column of antique art, or some con- sular statue of the imperial republic, wrapped in its marble robes, grandly beautiful in the simple dignity and unity of a faultless proportion.

Mr. Speaker, death extinguished a great light when Mr. CRISP died. He was not an orator like Clay, nor a logician like Webster, nor a metaphysician like Calhoun, yet he possessed in harmonious combination in a great degree all of these distinguishing attributes, and was, sir, the

best-rounded character I ever knew.   He was a pleasing, a
charming speaker; graceful in manner, clear in statement,
fair in his representation of his opponent's position and
argument, and candid in his search for the truth.

He knew how to be at the same time a partisan and a
patriot.   He was a partisan, because he believed that the
principles and policy of his party involved the highest
interest of his country and his race.   He was a patriot,
because he recognized in the beneficent Constitution and
institutions of his country the world's last and best hope
for constitutional liberty and free representative government.   He was no specialist, but he stood among the first
in all things which go to make greatness.   He was a wise
counselor, an able statesman, an eloquent advocate, an
accomplished parliamentarian, a courtly gentleman, and a
true friend.   His life is an inspiration to the young men
who are to come after him—a beacon light to guide them
to a higher sense of public duty, and give them a more
exalted idea of unselfish patriotism.   I do not care to dwell
at length upon the public career of the illustrious dead,
because it is a part of the history of the country and
familiar to all.   His name is indissolubly associated with
all the events of importance which have occurred in the
last decade.

From the time when, a mere youth, he first entered public
life, down to the moment when death called him from us,
his career was a series of brilliant successes.   As solicitor-
general, judge, president of conventions, member of Congress, Speaker, everywhere and at all times, he met every
obligation and discharged the duties of every trust committed to him with honesty, fidelity, and ability.   Right
here, upon the floor of this House, was the scene of his
greatest triumphs—his most brilliant achievements.   Cool,

self-poised, and well-balanced, he could always husband his resources at the right time and direct his energies with the best possible effect. Never did he develop his matchless powers or show his wonderful resources so well as when leading the forlorn hope of the minority; amid the fire and clash of party contention he would always parry the blows of the opposition, and by well-directed aims send his own darts with fatal precision into the heart of the enemy. He never voluntarily gave offense, and frequently disarmed opposition by his kindness and urbanity. Those, however, who met him in debate found that "there were blows to take as well as blows to give."

Some men may have surpassed Mr. CRISP in the subtle forces of thought; others may have excelled him in the divine gift of eloquence; still others may have been his equal in soundness of judgment and the judicial fairness with which he exercised power, and perhaps he had his peers in the high social qualities for which he was so eminently distinguished, but men possessing all these high attributes in combination are rarely found. Mr. CRISP possessed them all. His was a clean, active, incisive intellect. He was a fluent and eloquent speaker, an upright and impartial judge, an able and faithful Representative, a ready and skillful parliamentarian, and as a Speaker of this House for ability and fairness he goes into history the peer of Blaine and Randall. He was a polished and courtly gentleman, genial in manner and spirit as an "incense-breathing morn" in May, a bold and fearless antagonist, a faithful and confiding friend, and more than this, than these, than all, he was that "noblest work of God, an honest man." His was—

> One of the few, the immortal names,
> That were not born to die.

Mr. CRISP sent the sunshine of joy and gladness into the hearts of those who came in contact with his magnetic presence. It has been said that he never lost a friend nor made an enemy. Those of us who enjoyed the pleasure of comradeship with this golden-hearted man, who luxuriated, as it were, in the bright light of his genial companionship, can attest how great is our loss, how sad our bereavement. A gentler, kindlier heart never beat within a human breast. Would that I could speak of him in fitting language as a friend. He was my friend in all that term can suggest, and my personal loss is greater than I can tell. I loved him and I loved to follow where he led. But above all I loved to sit and hold sweet converse with him.

He has departed from among us, and we will never see his like again. Silently and sorrowfully he was laid away in the bosom of the Commonwealth he loved so well and served so faithfully. The grief of thousands of stricken hearts followed his funeral train. We have embalmed him in our hearts forever, and Georgia continues to weep upon the new-made grave of her best beloved son. Friend of my life—

> Farewell; my lips may wear a careless smile,
> My words may breathe the very soul of lightness,
> But the touched heart must deeply feel the while
> That life has lost a portion of its brightness.

Mr. CRISP was ambitious, "that glorious fault of angels and gods." He had ambition for official position not for its empty honors and perishing emoluments, but for the privilege and opportunity it gave him to serve his country. His ambition was neither selfish nor inordinate. He was ambitious to do the most good within the compass of a life's duration, and to that end he consecrated the best energies of his great mind and his honest heart. He wanted to go to the Senate, the sine qua non of every statesman's ambition, but his desire to attain this exalted station did not overcome his fixed purpose to serve his country where he could do his country most good. While we can not say of him what Antony said of Julius Cæsar, "I thrice presented him a kingly crown, which he did thrice refuse," yet we all do know that he was once presented with a seat in the American Senate and that he did once refuse it, because his friends and his party thought he could render the country greater service by remaining Speaker of this House, and with him their wish was law. He was assured by the present able and patriotic junior Senator from Georgia [Mr. Bacon], who was at the time an aspirant for the position, that if he would accept the appointment to the office of Senator tendered him by Governor Northen, made vacant by the death of the beloved and lamented Colquitt, he would have no opposition for the succession before the legislature; therefore his acceptance at that time meant the fulfillment of the cherished ambition of his life. Yet he made the personal sacrifice for the public good. Some men are stimulated to great achievements by the love of glory, others by the thirst for power, but the sentiment that absorbed the thought and thrilled the heart of Mr. CRISP was love of country.

> Breathes there the man with soul so dead
> Who never to himself hath said,
> This is my own, my native land!

The greatest heroes of the world's history are those who fought the battles against self and conquered. Mr. CRISP did this. He fought this fight, he kept the faith, he gained the victory, and wears the crown.

Pure and unselfish patriotism was his distinguishing characteristic.

Mr. Speaker, Georgia, ever proud of the achievements of her sons, looked upon this her favorite with peculiar pride and fondness, and her people, unforgetful of the sacrifices he had made for them, with a unanimity unsurpassed, had named him for the highest position within her gift, when his great heart ceased to beat. And thus this light was extinguished in the very blaze of his greatest political triumph; he reached forth his hand to take the Senatorial toga and grasped a shroud.

Mr. Speaker, as the stars go down to rise on some fairer shore, so our friend passes through the gloom of the grave to another and immortal condition of life. To those annealed in the blood of the crucified Galilean, there is no death.

> There is no death! What seems so is transition;
>   This life of mortal breath
> Is but a suburb of the life elysian,
>   Whose portal we call Death.

Divine revelation flashes from the sheen of the cross upon the darkness of the grave, the light of life, and anchors the broken heart of humanity, by the cable of faith, to the cherished truths of the resurrection and immortality. The religion of Christianity offers the only rational solution of the problems of life and death. We shall meet our friend and associate again, with all those who have preceded us.

> We may not sunder the veil apart,
>   That hides from our vision the gates of day.
> We only know that their barks no more
>   May sail with us o'er life's stormy sea;
> Yet somewhere, I know, on the unseen shore,
>   They watch and beckon and wait for me.

Our distinguished colleague and beloved friend was as felicitious in death as he was successful in life. He had lived long and well in a few brief years. He had served his country well and faithfully in positions of high trust and great honor. He was in the high tide of matured intellectual manhood, and in the noonday splendors of national fame. Age had not palsied his great powers, disappointment had not paled the star of his hope, nor frozen the current of his love. His work well done, his fame assured as part of his country's history, he "wraps the drapery of his couch about him and lies down to pleasant dreams," with every flower on his tomb wet with a nation's tears.

ADDRESS OF MR. LIVINGSTON.

Mr. LIVINGSTON. Mr. Speaker, when I first knew CHARLES FREDERICK CRISP, he was a very, very young man. He had been appointed solicitor-general of one of the circuits in the State of Georgia, and so well and so faithfully did he perform his duties as solicitor that when he asked an appointment to the judgeship of the same circuit, he received it at the hands of the governor. So well did he perform the duties of judge—no stain, no criticism, no slander was cast upon him or his administration—that at the end of his first term he was elected by the Georgia legislature for a second term.

In all his life he performed his duties well. Beginning without much of this world's goods, with but few friends, and with a limited education, he learned to trust implicitly in that old adage that—

> Honor and shame from no condition rise;
> Act well your part, there all the honor lies.

From his early manhood until the day of his death he was a practical, upright, honest official in every capacity, whether State or national.

In 1883 we had a very noted political contest, such as had not taken place for many years in Georgia. There was opposition to the nomination and election of the then acting governor, and there was a combination to beat him. There were, I believe, four or five candidates who were prominent. Two of them were very nearly equal, and controlling almost the entire vote of the convention. Mr.

CRISP was a delegate at that time in behalf of a man who had but 13 votes in the convention. I was a delegate, and when we met, the great question to solve was who should act as the permanent president of that convention. Neither of the dominant candidates could afford to allow his rival to name the presiding officer. There was a committee of thirteen appointed to suggest a presiding officer, and I am glad that I had the pleasure, as a member of that committee, of suggesting Mr. CRISP, and of stating in the committee room that, of all the men who were accredited as delegates to that convention on that day, Mr. CRISP was, in my humble opinion, one of the fairest-minded and most impartial and honest men in the convention. The suggestion was accepted; he was elected, and well and satisfactory did his selection prove to all interested parties. That was the beginning of his political life.

Mr. Speaker, so much has been said of Mr. CRISP to-day, both as to his life and as to his character, and the day has worn so far away and there are so many others who are anxious to say something in his behalf, that I shall only consume a moment or two more of time. I was with him much during the last year. I have been intimate with him for many years. I have seen him in sunshine and under the clouds. I have seen him in prosperity and in adversity, but never in all my life did I see Mr. CRISP so sorely tried as during the last year. When he thought of entering the race for United States Senator before the people of Georgia, the proposition was that this question should be remanded to the people, by primaries that should select the name of the Senator, believing that the Georgia legislature would indorse their action. It is well remembered by everybody on the floor of the House that a very strong man—a young man, strong in mind and in body—met him on the hustings in Georgia, contesting his claim to the Senatorship on account of his financial views.

It was intimated when Mr. CRISP left the field and failed to fill the engagements on hand, that it was for other reasons than his physical condition. He was criticised by the papers at home in some instances and by newspapers abroad. No one knew but Mr. CRISP his real condition. No physician who had attended him or prescribed for him knew his sufferings and the peculiar condition physically under which he labored. He withdrew. He submitted to those adverse criticisms and talked to me about it more than once. I was with him, Mr. Speaker, when he made his last speech on earth. Called by the people of Rome, Ga., and the surrounding country last fall to deliver a political speech, he had a magnificent audience, and never in my life did I see a speaker who nerved himself so thoroughly to do his full duty and measure up to his full capacity as did Mr. CRISP on that occasion. It was painful to see the effort he made to meet the expectations of the vast crowd that was hanging upon his lips. Yet he partially failed; it was his last effort. He only talked for a few minutes, and had to sit down. There were but few, perhaps including Mr. CRISP himself, who were aware of how fatal the malady was or would be, and how soon it would take him from his sphere of action.

Permit me to say in conclusion, Mr. Speaker, that his death was a national loss, but a much greater loss to Georgia, and to his home circle and to his personal friends an irreparable loss. He was an honest man, a good man, a discreet man, a wise man, a kind man, a liberal man, a manly man.

ADDRESS OF MR. LAWSON.

Mr. LAWSON. Mr. Speaker, on the 23d day of October last the soul of CHARLES FREDERICK CRISP, a great Georgian and an honored member of this body, passed through the gates of death into the presence of God. On that day his eyes rested for the last time on the autumnal splendors of his Southern skies. At such a season life is precious. For no artist, however deep his inspiration or exalted his imagination, has ever conceived a picture that rivaled in beauty and grandeur the surpassing loveliness of forest and landscape when "every leaf is an opal, and every tree a bower of varied beauty." From such a scene the soul of Mr. CRISP, conscious of its impending voyage and with no loved one absent, fearlessly launched upon the serene and placid sea of eternity. The places that knew him once will know him no more forever. But in a potent sense he still lives—lives in the virtues which he illustrated and in the successes which he achieved. These are invulnerable to the leaden scepter.

For the emulation of youth a nobler example than our deceased friend can scarcely be presented. Ardent, courageous, patriotic, and loyal to his adopted State, he, at the age of 16 years, grasped the sword in defense of her sovereign rights. Through four years of fatigue, hardships, and untold privations he followed the immortal Lee, the incomparable soldier and peerless citizen, amid the vicissitudes of fortune, to his final defeat. Then, at the age of 20 years, located in a small south Georgia town, he began a new life. A stranger, without either fortune or ancestral distinction, he began that long civic combat which, protracted through many years, ended only with his life. There was nothing in the physical aspect of the country, nor in its social and political condition, to animate the buoyancy of his youthful spirits or to guide him to an elevated plain of manhood and usefulness. Physical desolation all around and a thorough social upheaval, united with a galling oppression from without, tended to make the prospect cheerless and hopeless. But that manly courage and hardihood acquired in his soldier life qualified him for the conquest of adverse conditions and for his final triumph over all discouragements.

His education was meager, such only as he had acquired in the common schools; yet he was inducted into the learned profession of the law, a profession which in his Southern home had always held aloft the highest standards of learning, integrity, and honor. But, by dint of native ability, strenuous effort, and unfailing industry, he soon won a firm foothold in the profession, and was promoted to the office of solicitor-general, and charged with the prosecution of all infractions of the criminal laws in his circuit. His able and faithful discharge of the duties of his office is evidenced by the fact that on the first opportunity thereafter he was elected one of the judges of the superior courts of the State, courts which are vested with the highest original civil and criminal jurisdiction. Responsibilities of the most grave and onerous nature now devolved on him—none could be more so. To hold the scales of justice evenly between the contending animosities and passions of personal strifes, and to determine the issues of life and death impartially according to law, is a responsibility and a duty more exacting of the intelligence, the patience, the integrity, and the humanity of the judge than can otherwise be imposed.

Yet Mr. CRISP bore this burden with fortitude, with a sound understanding, and with conscientious loyalty to justice and fidelity to the State, eminently displaying in all emergencies the immovable and calm equipoise of an impartial magistrate.

His countrymen, to attest their approval of his able judicial administration, transferred him to a sphere of less serious responsibilities, but of higher honor and wider usefulness. They elected him to the Congress of the United States. I will not undertake to portray his labors and successes here. That will be much better done by his colaborers and contemporaries.

I did not witness any part of his Congressional career until he was chosen Speaker of the House of Representatives. As his colleague, and representing in part the same people, I witnessed, with a pardonable exhilaration of feeling, the industry, aptitude, ability, and fairness with which he deported himself in that great office. Quick to perceive, prompt to act, resolute of purpose, calm, composed, and suave in manner, he was a model officer. The stormy ebullition of partisan fury did not appall him, nor did sudden parliamentary entanglements disconcert him. Deliberate, just, self-poised, courteously according equal consideration to political friend and foe, he pursued the even tenor of his way. His personal bearing, and the unique blending of his moral and intellectual qualities, fitting him well and equally for action or for the council board, plainly marked him for the leadership of his party in the House. His sagacity, if not unerring, was of the keenest description. For these reasons, when his party suffered defeat, and when he descended from the chair to the floor of the House, party leadership was accorded him spontaneously, without rivalries, and without criticisms or comparisons. And though he knew that disease was corrupting the fountains of life, and though, haggard and wasted in strength, he sometimes seemed to bend beneath the burden, he resolutely maintained his station at the head of the column. Thus, as lawyer, jurist, legislator, Speaker, and statesman, he was a conspicuous figure and filled a large space in the public eye. His was—

> Th' applause of listening senates to command,
> And read his history in a nation's eyes.

Cut down in the midst of his years, in the prime and maturity of manhood, in the zenith of his fame and usefulness, his death is an irreparable loss to his State and country.

It may be remarked that his history was complete as it progressed. He advanced step by step from one degree of honor and usefulness to a higher, but every inch traversed was thoroughly conquered ground, and he did not need the brilliancy of a later achievement to reflect back and supplement or amend the deficiencies, the errors, or the failures of an earlier period.

One event in his political career stands out as a conspicuous illustration of his self-sacrificing patriotism. It was well known to his friends, and a fact which he did not hesitate to admit, that he coveted a seat in the United States Senate. That seemed to be the goal of his ambition, the capstone to an unbroken series of political conquests. But when, on the death of Senator Colquitt, the governor of Georgia offered to fill the vacancy in the Senate by the appointment of Mr. CRISP, he patriotically put aside the coveted prize, esteeming the services he was performing as Speaker of the House of Representatives to be of far greater value to the country than his services as a Senator.

His countrymen warmly appreciated and applauded his self-denial, and in the fullness of time, when he could accept the office without a sacrifice of duty, they, with practical unanimity in a primary election, indicated him as their choice for the Senatorship. All that remained to consummate the people's choice and his own ambition was the vote of the general assembly, which would have been cast before the passing of those beautiful October days. Had death spared him a few days longer, an admiring people would have crowned him with the laurels long coveted. But he is gone; and the glittering prize which, like ripened fruit, was just dropping into his hands, has fallen to the lot of another.

I can not close this brief sketch without some reference to the private and unofficial life of the honored dead. I will not profane the sanctuary of his domestic life by any allusion to it except to say that he was a loving, dutiful, and indulgent husband and father. No man's life is faultless. No man's life is as good as he wishes it to be and strives to make it. Life is a drama of alternate defeat and victory. The private life of Mr. CRISP, leaving out the foibles and follies that human nature in the best of men is heir to, was untarnished and spotless. No one ever questioned his integrity, and no suspicion or slander ever cast a film upon the clear surface of his character. It was above reproach. His affable manners and singularly democratic habits drew men to him and "grappled them with hooks of steel." No aspersion of his political foes ever escaped his lips; they even shared the beneficence of his Christian charity. His bonhommie was perennial; his cheerfulness a never-failing stream. It was a delight to share in the pleasantries of his sunny disposition. As greatness grew upon him he did not

forget his early and less-favored friends. The great poet
tells us that—

> 'Tis a common proof,
> That lowliness is young ambition's ladder,
> Whereto the climber upward turns his face;
> But when he once attains the upmost round,
> He then unto the ladder turns his back,
> Looks in the clouds, scorning the base degrees
> By which he did ascend.

Not so with Mr. CRISP. A friend once gained was a
friend forever. The friends of his early days were the
stancher friends of his last days. The period of his suffering and decline was wreathed in their admiration and love.
And if any sacrifice which they could have offered could
have beaten back the stealthy and relentless approach of
the grim monster, he to-day, strong and militant, would be
an active leader among us.

I conclude with one other remark. Death came to him
as it comes to but few. It did not with a sudden and resist-
less stroke mercifully cut him down. It did not, through
wasting disease, always nearing the inevitable end, assure
him that recovery was impossible. But it tantalized him
with alternate hope and dread. Now it approached; again
it receded; but the dread Reaper was ever dimly present.
In the noisy altercations of these Halls, in the privacy of
his home, in the council chamber, on the highway, in the
hall of assemblies, in solitude, in society, at funerals and
at marriage feasts, everywhere and always, Death, toying
with his heartstrings, mocked him. Whether his end was
near or far off, he knew not; but he did know that his sleep-
less enemy was inexorable and relentless. For months he
stood near and listened to the lashing of the waves upon
the eternal shore and feared not. Surely the valiant never
taste of death but once.

ADDRESS OF MR. MORSE.

MR. MORSE. Mr. Speaker, at this late hour I promise that my words will be very few. The great dramatist has said:

> All the world's a stage,
> And all the men and women merely players.

Of this, Washington, with its ever-changing life, seems to me to be a fit illustration. I often think, as I ascend the steps of this Capitol building, of all the men who have served here and walked these streets, ascended these steps and had their little day of honor, fame, and pleasure, and have joined the silent majority.

CHARLES FREDERICK CRISP, in whose honor we have met here this afternoon, like all the rest, is but an illustration, to quote from Gray's immortal Elegy in a Country Churchyard, that—

> The paths of glory lead but to the grave.

These considerations should lead us to look away to that undiscovered country, should lead us to seek for honor and treasure laid up "where neither moth nor rust doth corrupt, and where thieves do not break through nor steal." How it should lead us to strive for that incorruptible crown of glory that fadeth not away, for those enduring honors that will stand when the marble crumbles, when the bronze turns to dust, and when the canvas fades—will stand when the elements have melted with fervent heat and the works thereof are burned up.

Mr. Speaker, to know Mr. CRISP was to love the man. I disagreed with this distinguished statesman upon nearly every political question, upon economic and financial questions, but I am here to bear testimony to the fact that I believe he was a thoroughly honest and sincere man. I am here to say that he was a refined and courteous gentleman; and I am here to say that he bore the duties of that great office which you enjoy, Mr. Speaker, and whose responsibilities you know so well—I am here to say that he bore those great honors with a quiet modesty and dignity. Mr. CRISP was a gentleman in the widest, broadest sense of those words. Shakespeare says:

> The evil that men do lives after them;
> The good is oft interred with their bones.

I have often thought when reading that, that he spoke ironically. I think exactly the opposite is true. I think we love to recount the virtues of our deceased friends rather than their failings and faults. The distinguished gentleman from Pennsylvania [Mr. Dalzell] has said that Speaker CRISP had faults; but he has truly and justly said that his virtues far outshone them; his gentleness, his culture, his urbanity of manner, even to his political opponents as well as his friends, was a marked characteristic of this great man, who now sleeps in the soil of his own loved State, the great Empire State of Georgia.

Mr. Speaker, Mr. CRISP died in the zenith of his fame. He died at the post of duty, as one should wish to die. You remember, Mr. Speaker, when the surgeons gathered around Mr. Garfield in the depot when he was stricken down by the vilest assassin that ever cursed the earth, he asked Dr. Bliss: "Doctor, is the wound mortal?" And you remember the answer that the doctor made. Said he: "Mr. Garfield, we fear the worst." And that great man said: "Doctor, I am not afraid to die." Why not? Because he was at the post of duty. One of my illustrious and distinguished predecessors, who for sixteen years represented in yonder Hall the district which I have the honor to represent—John Quincy Adams, the Old Man Eloquent—died in yonder Hall in 1848. He died as he lived—at the post of duty, like this man. He died on his shield, and his last words were: "This is the last of earth. I am content." Surely the place where a statesman would wish to die!

Some of the oldest people who live in my country will tell you that their grandparents told them about a dark day. It occurred on the 19th day of May, 1780. It began to grow dark at 10 o'clock in the morning, and at noon it was so dark in New England that people could not see to read out of doors. Our fathers had very few books besides the Bible, and in that book they read that God had appointed a day in which He would judge the world. Very many of the good people of New England thought the Day of Judgment was at hand. Indeed, Mr. Speaker, as you know, the strange phenomenon has never been explained. The only explanation ever offered was that the smoke from dense forest fires in the West met a dense fog from the East. At any rate, on the 19th day of May, 1780, at noonday in New England a man could not see to read out of doors. This dark day overtook the Connecticut house of assembly in session ; and amid profound silence and gloom one of the members arose in his place and said:

Mr. Speaker, it is evident that some strange and wonderful providence of Almighty God is upon us, by which we can not see to read at noon time. It may be, sir, that the Day of Judgment is at hand. In view of this strange and wonderful providence of God, I move you, sir, that the Connecticut house of assembly do now adjourn.

There was another member of the house of assembly, whose name was Abraham Davenport, and he was a Quaker; and he stood up in his place and opposed the motion. He said:

Mr. President, I am opposed to the motion to adjourn. I am utterly unable to explain the darkness. It may be that some strange and wonderful providence of God is upon us. It may be, as my brother has said, that the Day of Judgment is at hand. But, sir, as I know of no better place to be overtaken by death and the judgment than at the post of duty, I move you, sir, that the candles be brought in and the act be read again.

It was done; and the business of the house went on.

Now, Mr. Speaker, I have faith to believe that if you and I, like CHARLES F. CRISP, and John Quincy Adams, and James Abram Garfield, and Abraham Davenport, are found at the post of duty, in the largest meaning of those words, having our peace made with God, we need not fear death or the judgment. Surely this man died at the post of duty; he died bravely and he sleeps well; his name and his memory and his record will be revered by his countrymen to the remotest time. Fare you well, CHARLES F. CRISP! We shall see you no more on the shores of time. We say to you a last and sad farewell.

ADDRESS OF MR. TUCKER.

Mr. TUCKER. Mr. Speaker, in the death of CHARLES FREDERICK CRISP the country has lost a valuable statesman, the Democratic party one of its most loyal and efficient leaders, the State of Georgia one of her most devoted sons, and his family an affectionate husband and father. The qualities of mind and traits of character which distinguished him in this Hall have been amply portrayed as well by his political friends as by his adversaries. They were of no mean caliber, and history will accord to Mr. CRISP a high and honorable place in the long catalogue of distinguished American statesmen.

The province of eulogy too often runs into the extravagant; but a just tribute to our friend need not exceed the bounds of truth in according him a high and honorable position among the great leaders of his party. I would not claim for him the powers of analysis of a Calhoun, or the ponderous eloquence of a Webster, or the masterful, imperious leadership of a Clay, or the brilliant dash of a Blaine; but combining, it may be in a lesser degree, many of the strongest qualities of each, with a coolness of judgment and equipoise of mind which has rarely been equaled, he made available his powers, and all of them, in the discharge of public duties, as effectively as any man I have ever seen in public life. If he was not so great a logician as Mr. Calhoun, his powers of logic were always thoroughly available, and wielded with telling force against his adversary.

If he lacked the highest type of eloquence, his intense earnestness in debate supplied what the rhetorical art might have suggested. His leadership was always won by the arts of persuasion rather than by arbitrary dogmatism. He was one of the most resourceful as well as forceful men in the maintenance of his position in debate that has appeared in this Hall for years. Few men possessed the power of drawing upon their resources and utilizing their every power in action as did Mr. CRISP.

His manners were simple, unostentatious, and cordial. A natural playfulness of spirit, united with a dignity and a self-reliance of character, repelled none who sought his counsel, and drew the closer to him all who sought his society. He did not hesitate to lend his ready counsel in molding the policy of his party nor did he shirk the responsibility which rested upon him as one of its trusted leaders. As a leader on the floor or as Speaker he was always bold, aggressive, and oftentimes defiant. The elements of character in him were harmonized in a certain simplicity of style which offended no man's self-love and commanded the respect and confidence of all.

It was not always my fortune to agree with him as to matters of party policy, and in the memorable fight for the Speakership in the Fifty-second Congress I felt it my public duty, against my personal inclination, to advocate the claims of another. Such action on my part, however, so far as I know, never created any breach in our personal friendship.

The State of Virginia has always felt the deepest interest in the life and career of Mr. CRISP. In those days which tried men's souls he freely spilled his blood on her soil, and from May, 1861, until May, 1864, when Virginia was "a looming bastion fringed with fire," he mingled with her people, enlisted with her sons, and fought by their

sides. As a soldier, Mr. CRISP exhibited the highest qualities of excellence. With a cheerful temper, he bore the
privations of war in the camp, on the field, or on the march,
and he was ever obedient to command, and ready to respond
to his country's call.

He enlisted at Luray, in the Valley of Virginia, in
Company K of the Tenth Virginia Infantry, while his
father and his brother Harry enlisted in an artillery company in the county of Shenandoah. He served first under
Col. S. A. Gibbons in the brigade of the gallant Elzey,
afterwards commanded by Gen. W. H. Taliaferro (now
Judge Taliaferro), of Gloucester County, Va., and subsequently commanded by Gen. George H. Stewart.

In speaking of his services as a soldier, his old captain,
Capt. R. S. Parks, of Luray, Va., says :

In the spring of 1862 our regiment was transferred from Joe
Johnston's command on the Rappahannock to Jackson's command in the Valley, and remained in that command until the
sun set at Appomattox. Most of the regiment was captured
with Ed Johnson's division in the "bloody salient" on the 11th
of May, 1864, where perhaps occurred the fiercest struggle and
more blood was spilled than at any place during the war.
CRISP was captured at that time and was not released until
after the war. He enlisted at the age of 16 years as a private,
and was second lieutenant when he was captured. He was
quite small, not disposed to be corpulent, as he grew to be in
after life. He was very quiet and unobtrusive ; in fact, retiring
in his manner; a great reader, he was never without a book.
He carried one in his knapsack always, if he had one (but
"Jackson's Foot Cavalry" did not like to carry superfluous
baggage), or in his blanket. Often when the regiment was
halted to rest on the march, he would immediately sit down
and read from his book. He had a most remarkable memory,
and could read a book and then relate everything in it, giving
in many instances the exact language.

Like all the members of Company K, he was a soldier from head to foot, for no man ever commanded a better set of men or harder fighters than those who composed that company. Taps for "lights out" have been heard by many since 1865, and one by one they are passing to the other shore. Each one, so far as I have seen or heard, drew the drapery of death around him as coolly as he wrapped himself in his own blanket and laid down to sleep and dream on the field of carnage to await the call to arms at early dawn.

In the infantry there was little chance for promotion for gallant service. They were under orders, and had only to fight and die on the heights of Gettysburg, in the tanglewood of the Wilderness, or the swamps of the Chickahominy. CHARLIE was a soldier without a stain, a statesman without guile, and in war and peace a gentleman.

The people of Virginia, in common with those of the whole country, mourn at the grave of their friend, defender, and protector, and claim the privilege through her Representatives here of placing a flower upon his open grave in commemoration of their lasting gratitude for his fidelity to her and to his country.

ADDRESS OF MR. HOOKER.

Mr. HOOKER. Mr. Speaker, it was my pride and good fortune to enjoy the friendship of CHARLES FREDERICK CRISP, and I feel a better man for having been allowed that inestimable privilege.

The more than ordinary solemnity of this sad occasion deeply impresses me, and I am fully cognizant of my utter incompetency to add anything to the remarks that have already been so feelingly, justly, and appropriately made; yet I am unwilling to let this opportunity pass without paying my heartfelt tribute to him whose memory we honor to-day.

My acquaintance with him began at the beginning of the Fifty-second Congress, when he had just been honored by his party as its candidate for the Speakership, and I look back upon my short political career and my heart teems with gratitude to our lamented friend for the many words of counsel and encouragement which his benevolent and generous nature prompted him to bestow upon those who sought his aid and advice.

Among the prominent characteristics of this leader among men I would call attention to one that particularly stands forth when observing his eminent career, and that is the universal and kindly consideration which he extended to the younger and less experienced members of this body.

However burdened with the cares of a busy public life, he was always ready to listen to the appeals of his younger colleagues and give them the assistance of his masterly mind, so rich in experience, so trained in the affairs of legislation.

Time alone will disclose the true wisdom of his course; and though he has departed, his memory will be treasured in the hearts of all who have been associated with this noble character.

He was a careful and conscientious legislator, yet so strong in his convictions, when once formed, that he followed the lines of duty as he saw them with untiring zeal and energy.

His pluck and perseverance soon gained for him distinction, and the party whose principles he espoused quickly recognized him as a leader, and he was ever afterwards a prominent figure in its affairs.

Strong partisan that he was, he never forgot the rights of others. Honored as he was by the unbounded confidence of his fellow-men, he never denied to others the consideration due them.

Though many of us differed with him on the leading political issues of the day, yet we admired this progressive, resolute, national figure, who played so important a part in many of the leading events of recent years.

Simple, courteous in manner, forcible in expression, fearless in conflict, the virtues and qualities of this distinguished servant, faithful, upright, honorable, raised him to the pinnacle of high esteem in the minds and hearts of his fellow-countrymen.

His private and public career furnish a most noble example to the American youth endeavoring to attain laudable ambition, and to those of the older generation who may be discouraged and disheartened an inspiration to an awakened and renewed activity.

ADDRESS OF MR. BARTLETT.

Mr. BARTLETT. Mr. Speaker, to those distinguished gentlemen who have spoken and who will address the House on this sad occasion, and whose gifted tongues are so well aided by a long and familiar association with him in these Halls, might well be left the fit memorial of this our late colleague and honored friend. To me the effort to speak of the life and death of him whose memory we memorialize to-day is difficult indeed, for my tongue almost refuses to convey into speech what my heart feels, and it is with much distrust of myself that I have ventured to speak at all; indeed, it is with an emotion that almost stifles utterance I approach the altar of his hallowed memory to lay upon it my simple flower of feeble tribute. I shall not attempt to relate in detail the various epochs in his illustrious career, nor to delineate the many admirable and exalted virtues he possessed. That will be done by others more able and eloquent than myself.

Mr. Speaker, again has Death invaded this House—again with relentless greed has borne a trophy from our ranks. Again we pause amid the busy scenes of public duties to pay tribute to the dead. This time the insatiate Archer has hurled his shaft with unerring and fatal precision at one of its brightest and most shining marks, and not only this House, but this whole Union, has lost one of its loveliest and purest ornaments. The mind in which genius and real worth had already erected a temple to fame and usefulness, and which but awaited the opportunity, already at hand, to make it grander, greater, and more useful, is no more; the heart in which the noblest virtues dwelt is stopped forever. The Representative of his people on this floor, who was soon to bear the commission of his State as a member of the Senate of the United States, has ended his earthly career and taken up his abode in the "silent halls of death."

With bowed heads and sorrowing hearts, but with sweet and hallowed recollections of his life, his friendship, and association, we stand to-day over the new-made grave of CHARLES FREDERICK CRISP.

On the 23d of October last the reluctant wires conveyed to the world the sad intelligence that Mr. CRISP, for many years a member of this House, twice its presiding officer, was dead.   A great bereavement fell upon my State and upon the whole people—a sudden and most untimely bereavement. The blow went straight to the heart of the great State he represented on this floor, and Georgia laments the loss more than words can express.   "The flower of her hope withered" because the new and highest honor in her gift, prepared for him by the almost unanimous voice of her people, remained unbestowed by her hands.

He died when but little advanced beyond the prime of life. His success had been equal to that of the favored ones of the day.   He left us at a time when the past yielded a great deal for gratifying retrospection, when the present afforded the richest elements of happiness, and the future invited him to higher honors and ampler resources of enjoyment, and assured him success in a field of greater usefulness for his State and the people of this great Government.   But all that he possessed, all that he hoped for, could not stay the hand of the great destroyer.

Mr. CRISP filled many important positions, and he met and performed the duties of each in a manly, straightforward, honest way. As a young volunteer soldier in the cause of the Confederate States, he was brave, determined, and obedient to authority. He was a member of the legal profession, a profession which is "as ancient as magistracy, as noble as virtue, as necessary as justice," and which, above all others, shapes and fashions the institutions under which we live ; a profession "which is generous above all others, and in which living merit in its day is bestowed according to its deserts." As a member of the bar of the southwestern circuit of Georgia, a bar noted at all times for the learning and ability of its members, he soon forced his way to the front rank, and at an early period after entering practice was appointed solicitor-general of that judicial circuit.

As a lawyer, while he always represented the interest of his client, he never undertook to mislead judge or jury by specious sophistry, but he adhered to the same scrupulous sincerity in his advocacy of his client's cause which he observed in the other transactions of life. As prosecuting officer for the State, while he fearlessly pursued the viola-tors of the law, no innocent man, however poor or humble, was permitted to suffer.

He was judge of the superior court of his State, the court of the highest jurisdiction, other than the supreme court of the State, for the correction of errors of law. Though quite a young man when he was made judge, and with somewhat limited experience at the bar, he soon proved himself to be an ideal judge. He was patient and courte-ous, not given to that vice possessed by some judges, first to find that which he might in due time have heard from the bar. He never met the case halfway nor gave occasion to parties to say their counsel or proofs were not heard. His integrity was above even suspicion, and though the judgment may have been erroneous at times, the counsel and the parties knew that the law had been pronounced as he believed it to be—for at last, above all things, integrity is the portion and proper virtue of a judge.

Mr. CRISP's intellectual excellence and power were due to his very extraordinary common sense and an innate controlling impulse to know and do what was right. His mind was a distinctly judicial mind; his education was by no means thorough, because the years of his early youth were spent in the Confederate Army, and the time usually devoted to education was given in defense of the South and her cause. When he was appointed judge, he had had little experience at the bar, and that only as solicitor-general; yet when he was appointed judge, he soon took rank among the ablest of our judges, and became and was regarded one of the best, if not the best, in Georgia. His charges to the juries were models of clearness and directness of speech. He always "dug deep for the justice of the case," and when found, permitted no technicalities to defeat it. He belonged to that class of lawyers and judges who rely upon their clear perception of what is just and right and true rather than upon books and cases—more upon principle than precedents—

Juvat accedere fontes.

His mind was preeminently practical, and his oratory was in admirable keeping with his strong natural sense. He invariably spoke for use, and never for display. Mr. CRISP was of a most gentle and kindly disposition; he was an amiable man; the law of love dwelt in his heart, and the "milk of human kindness" mingled in his blood. His manners were the most bland and agreeable, and this, added to the intuitive quickness of his mind, exuberant

and good temper, his devotion to the truth, and attachment
to his friends made him the favorite he was with his brethren at the bar, his associates in this House, and the public.
Though ambitious to be distinguished and useful, he was
not in the slightest degree selfish. Those who did not
know him well or understand him might have supposed
that he was always on the alert to make friends for his
political purposes ; but the truth was he was so broad, so
catholic in his kindness and gratitude, that it was perfectly
natural for him to be more than merely courteous and
polite ; it was perfectly natural for him to compliment all
with whom he came in contact with his attentions and
courtesy.

> And thus he bore without abuse
> The grand old name of gentleman.

True, indeed, it is we can say of Mr. CRISP that he was
distinguished in the humbler walks of life by his devotion
to family and friends, by his simplicity in manner and
speech, and a warm welcome to all who approached him.

> His was a soul of honor everywhere,
> That to ignoble actions scorned to bend ;
> True to his trust in friendship's faith, he ne'er
> Forgot a favor or forsook a friend.

He possessed in a degree that is worthy of emulation by
us all "that humanity that meets in every man a brother;"
that sympathy which enters with warmth into the feelings of
others; that friendship which glows with generous emotions
and binds us to those we love with most indissoluble ties;
that charity that puts on every dubious action and appearance the most favorable interpretation; that philanthropy
that feels with quickness the distresses of others, and that
spirit of justice that accords to all their due.

Of his services in the Hall of Congress others have

spoken, and I will not endeavor to say more, except that as
a national character his fame stands out before the world
preeminently great. A man of broad, conservative views,
honest convictions, zealous in patriotic endeavor, courageous in the defense of right, gentle, modest, and merciful,
he stood above his compeers a statesman of the nation
and defender of the South and her people. He was never
recreant to a single trust. His love for home, his love for
Georgia and for the Union, and his bold stand for his people
against oppression of every character have won for him a
place in the hearts of his countrymen and among the
imperishable names in the Halls of Congress, where he was
the peer of his ablest opponent.

It may be and is true that he did not possess that brilliant
genius that marks a meteoric fame; but his was that worth
and ability that with steady glow grew brighter as it swept
into the sphere of usefulness. Though he has gone from
among us, though his warm, sympathetic heart will beat
no more, and though his body is beyond mortal view, his
name and fame are written among that constellation of the
great men of the South and of this Union, where it will
live on and on through the life of the Republic.

The great beauty of Mr. Crisp's character was his constant, tender, loving, and enthusiastic devotion to his wife
and children. His family life was, after all, his chiefest
grace. With a tender and gentle courtesy and with a loving nature, he lavished his heart's best gifts on her whom
God gave to him, and with a fond father's love and devotion he cherished the children who grew up around him.
No change that years and sickness wrought brought any
change in the gentleness, care, and love that were bestowed
upon the wife. Though sickness and affliction had made

the wife almost an invalid, yet upon her and to her he always bestowed all gentleness, all care, all devotion. To him, indeed, the afflicted wife seemed "dearer than the bride."

But neither his fame as a lawmaker nor love of his people nor the devotion and prayers of his loved one could stay the hand of the great destroyer. Silent and sure and remorseless, death heeds neither youth nor age; genius, learning, poverty, nor wealth; the tears of relatives and friends, nor the cold indifference of strangers. "All equally the universal reaper gathers to his ever-filling yet ever unfilled garner—the tomb."

On a calm, still Sabbath day, at deep twilight, with hands of reverent love, we laid him in the bosom of the universal mother, by the side of two of his children who had gone before, there to rest under Georgia's soil, beneath Southern skies and the city he loved so well and the section he served with so constant fidelity; there, where the shapely shafts of Parian white tell of the peace within, where the everlasting hills uplift their rugged crests to catch the first ray of the morning sun, symbols to the eye of faith of the glorious coming of the new dawn; there, in the company of son and daughter, he awaits the final destiny of greatness.

What a noble example has Mr. CRISP set to the young men of his State, of this great Union, of diligence in business, of truth and devotion to principle and justice, honesty and uprightness in all his conduct toward his fellow-men and in public life, which is the basis of our social connections. This was the means by which he achieved success in life; and here is an example on which our young men should be proud to form themselves, an example that refutes "the dull maxims of idleness and profligacy," and points

out the real road, and the only highway, in a Republic to
honor, fortune, and fame.

I utter no idle words when I say for the people of Georgia
that, "living, we all loved him; dead, we will cherish his
memory in our innermost hearts."

> His virtues he bequeathed us, that we yet
> May meet him in a lovelier land than this,
> Where darkness is unknown, suns never set,
> And sorrow never comes, but all is bliss.

Mr. Speaker, I append as part of my remarks the account
of the funeral services had at the church in Americus on
October 25, 1896, and the funeral oration delivered by his
old army commander, that distinguished Georgia divine,
Gen. C. A. Evans, the old commander of the "Stonewall
Brigade."

The church was reached at 2.30 p. m., around which had
assembled another vast crowd. It is a frame building of quaint
architecture. The vestibule has two large octagonal columns,
back of which is a deep recess. Round these two massive sup-
ports were entwining long folds of black crape, from chapiter
to plinth. Broad steps, the entire width of the church front,
led up from a gentle slope to the vestibule. The church is
embowered in a grove of oaks, which is inclosed by an old
fence. The very place has an air of solemnity; but the
occasion gave a deeper funereal aspect to the church and
surroundings.

VIEWED THE REMAINS.

An hour was allotted to those who desired to have a last look
at their friend and townsman. A single-file procession began,
and the entire time was consumed in this sad privilege. The
face, so familiar in life to all the people of Americus, still bore
the same calm, peaceful expressions that had won the hearts
and esteem of all who knew him. Pale though it was, still the
pallor of death had not robbed it of serenity nor of its former
lifelike semblance. Though his last words were, "Oh, what

pain!'' the features bespoke that calm resignation to God's will and the trust he had placed in his Creator's promise of salvation. Thus the people saw him, and thus his memory will be cherished.

The bells of the city were still pealing their requiem when the hour for the last sad rites arrived. The casket rested on a bier in front of the chancel, buried in beds of rarest flowers. The pulpit and other places were covered with floral emblems, donated by admirers of the deceased.

While the people were gathering into the church, the organ in softest notes pealed forth a funeral dirge. After this solemn rendition the choir sang, ''There is rest for the weary,'' so feelingly that many of the congregation shed tears.

Rev. T. M. Christian, of the First Methodist Church, then read the one hundred and third psalm, after which Rev. Leroy Henderson, pastor of the Presbyterian Church, read the thirteenth chapter of 1st Corinthians. Then Rev. Mr. Turpin, of the First Baptist Church, offered the following prayer:

''O God, beneath whose throne Thy people in all ages have dwelt secure, regard us in great compassion, we beseech Thee, for Thy hand hath touched us.

''O Thou who makest sore and bindest up, draw us with the cords of Thy love, for we are sorely smitten before Thee.

''Look in mercy upon a nation whose citizens are saying one to another: 'Know ye not that there is a prince and a great man fallen this day in Israel?'

''May the great loss we have sustained serve to rebuke the bitterness of party spirit and to calm the turbulent passions of the people.

''Visit with Thy salvation our public servants gathered here from different sections of our State and country, and profitably remind us all that 'the paths of glory lead but to the grave.' Help us to remember 'what shadows we are and what shadows we pursue.'

''Bless, we implore Thee, our community, which so deeply mourns the loss of her distinguished citizen, for we were accustomed to lean upon his words, and are fain to cry out:

''O fall'n at length that tower of strength
Which stood four-square to all the winds that blew!

"Lord God of all comfort, bind up the broken hearts of this family circle, whose bitter grief would almost make them say, 'Behold and see if there is any sorrow like unto our sorrow.'

"Strengthen with Thy might in the inner man Thy venerable servant, as he receives back under his fatherly protection to-day the daughter who in the days of her youth so confidingly gave her heart to him, who became so worthy of her unfaltering trust, but who has now, alas, been parted from her.

"We invoke, O God, Thy tenderest mercies upon our sister. O Thou who art the light of the world, abide with her, for Thou hast taken away from her the light of her eyes. May Thy everlasting arms be underneath her, and do Thou comfort, sustain, and keep her as she sighs—

"For the touch of a vanish'd hand,
And the sound of a voice that is still.

"Be merciful, O Lord, to all the members of the household. Sanctify to the bereaved sons and daughters their deep distress.

"Look down with Thine all-pitying eye upon Thy young servant, who so tenderly leaned upon her father's bosom, and who was such a joy to his heart. Hold not Thy peace at her tears. Lord God, bless these manly boys, and may the mantle of their father fall upon them.

"We praise thee, O God, that we 'sorrow not as those who have no hope.' We thank Thee for the belief of Thy servant who has finished his course in those Holy Scriptures which are able to make us wise unto eternal life, and for his simple trust in the Redeemer of the world. And we thank Thee that throughout his public career he ever 'wore the white feather of a blameless life.' For Thou hast taught us to ask: 'Who shall ascend into the hill of the Lord or who shall stand in His holy place?' and Thou hast said: 'He that hath clean hands and a pure heart; who hath not lifted up his soul unto vanity, nor sworn deceitfully.' Glory be to God for 'the hope, the blessed hope, when days and years are o'er, we all shall meet in Heaven,' where—

'The saints of all ages in harmony meet,
Their Saviour and brethren transported to greet,
While the anthems of rapture unceasingly roll,
And the smile of the Lord is the feast of the soul,

through Jesus Christ, who was delivered for our offenses, and was raised for our justification. Amen."

The choir then sang, "We shall sleep, but not forever." A stillness akin to death impressed the solemnity of the occasion upon every heart. The bereaved ones sat near the casket, having the sympathy of their friends from every section.

THE FUNERAL ORATION.

A moment of silence, and Georgia's noble old soldier and Mr. CRISP's warmest and truest friend, Gen. Clement A. Evans. stood in the presence of the dead to pay a tribute to his unblemished life and express sorrow at his early death. Following is the oration:

GENERAL EVANS'S ORATION.

A great bereavement has befallen a whole people—a sudden, sad, and most untimely bereavement. The strong, tender ties which bind men together in the closest relations of human life are sundered. I say most untimely, in reverent, humble submission to the good will of Almighty God. Death aimed his shaft at the brightest mark which for the moment shone upon the public field. With startling emphasis the quick stroke, ringing throughout the State, announced the imperial authority of the insatiate archer to strike down the most exalted human figure as surely and easily as to bring a sparrow to the ground.

Our State takes this blow to heart, for it has cut off her beloved son in his prime, and she laments the loss as Jacob mourned for Joseph. Her pride is wounded to the quick, for in him she had gloried as a valiant supporter of her fame. The flower of her hope withereth because the new and lustrous honor prepared for him by her sovereign will remains unbestowed by her hands. To-day Georgia embodies the sorrows of a great, sympathetic people, and by every token tells that a whole State can feel a common grief. Using the language of another, "We expect the sun to go down in the evening, we expect the flower to wither in the fall, we expect the stream to be frozen in the winter, but that the sun should go down at noon, that the flower should wither in the summer, that the stream of life should be frozen before the chill of age had come upon it, is a reflection that saddens the soul in man."

It is my sad duty in the present ministrations of this sanctuary to give some expression to this common sentiment and to speak of a noble life so thoroughly known as not to require minute description.

It is commonly commented on that the career of Mr. Crisp was a steadily ascending, uninterrupted rising from the first level on the shore line of a citizen's duty, upward from grade to grade, until he had reached that lofty table-land where all supreme distinctions become possible. Such a career illustrates the free course laid open by the peculiar principles of our American Union to honorable aspiration, as well as the wisdom of our political laws, which give to the people the privilege of a wide range in selecting their representatives and rulers. Without special prestige, without fortune, without the favoring gale of association formed by residence, and beginning business life obscurely in a little Georgia town as a returned soldier—a youth of 20—he enters on the work of life amidst the unfavorable conditions that prevailed in 1865 throughout this Southern land. The reflection has interested me personally that at this precise period we were not a day's ride on horse apart, both just returned from the same scenes, the same fields, possessing the same spirit, and looking alike landward from the shore line; behind us the sea where a nation had been wrecked; before us an unknown wilderness of political possibilities.

It is not on this warp, however, I would weave the suggestive event of his nobly successful life, but instead thereof I would point the young men of the State to the clean truth that Mr. Crisp attained his fame by industrious, honorable, and patriotic discharge of the duties devolved upon him from time to time. Few public men in Georgia have gained great distinction by their sole reliance upon the adventitious aid of fortune and ancestral name. That illustrious roll which we are proud to call is answered by a multitude of noble men who overcame disadvantage by the sweat of the brow, the throb of the brain, the tension of nerve, the pulse of heart—by men who "stopped the mouths of lions and quenched the violence of fire;" by men who patiently waited while they earnestly worked out their manifest

destiny, and who, in a heroic scorn of obstacles, achieved greatness in all those various departments of human endeavor open to
all men through the regulated liberties of our free land. Ambition requires no liaison with corruption in order to attain a
glorious fame. The path to human glory should be as "the
path of the just that groweth brighter unto the perfect day."
In the battle of life the aspirant for fame should indeed be a hero
in the strife, and if in the encounter he should go down, let it be
said of him at the roll call of human names, "He died on the
field of honor!"

The life of Mr. CRISP as a lawyer is above reproach. After
a year of preparation he was admitted to the bar, and then came
on six years of that experience which brings discouragement to
many young barristers and during which some unhappily pre-
destinate their total failure. But baffling, rather than being
baffled, and seizing opportunities as they moved within the circle
of his grasp, and rising by gradations which demanded and were
met by the toil that gains ascensions, the young lawyer of Ellaville became the solicitor-general of his judicial circuit, and after
four years' experience rose by appointment and elections to an
honorable and responsible position upon the bench of the superior court of Georgia.

Tested in these offices of delicate, difficult, and often embar-
rassing duties, Mr. CRISP won the esteem of the bar, satisfied
the demands of the law, proved himself an able, just, incorruptible judge, and increased his popularity as his intercourse with
the people widened.

The result was his transference from the bench to the Halls
of Congress, where services were rendered as occasions came,
which gained him increasing attention until even in a Congress
where he was at a disadvantage by being in the minority, and
especially because he represented a Southern district, he commanded such respect for his courage, his parliamentary skill,
his fidelity to his party, and his patriotic devotion to his country
that he was conceded the position of leader of his side of the
House. His field battles with the eminent Speaker—a foeman
worthy of his steel—will always be memorable parliamentary
history. Gallant as any chivalrous Southern knight, skilled
in the tactics of Congressional proceeding, ready in running

skirmish, and steady as a stone wall under assault, he stood
foremost among national party men on the floor of Congress
until the great change in the political situation gave his friends
the opportunity to reverse positions between himself and his able
antagonist by elevating him to the Speakership, one of the most
commanding offices created by the Constitution.   With many
other Georgians I have proudly witnessed in Washington the
contests and the triumphs of this conspicuous Representative
from our own State.   Recalling the old historic names of Georgia—recalling the days when Berrien charmed the Senate with
his pellucid speech, when Toombs in torrents of eloquence stirred
the House, when Stephens, like a river, made glad with limpid
logic the hearts of his countrymen, when Cobb, illustrious
from his youth, held the Speaker's gavel, and on to Hill the
superb, Brown the wise, and Colquitt the tribune, and others
who like these requited the State with fadeless luster for the
honors she had conferred on them—I say, recalling these historic men, I am not loath to place among them the name and
fame of the statesman whose loss from the national councils
we so sadly deplore.

I will venture to say that no more magnificent display of
political self-denial ever occurred in the lives of aspiring men
than that which shines out in splendor like the noonday sun in
one well-known event of Mr. CRISP's political life.   I refer, of
course, to the occasion when he put aside the Senatorial toga
proffered him by Governor Northen on the death of the lamented
Senator Colquitt.   I will not try your patience nor party fealty
by asking what you would have done.   Let us imagine that
others would have acted as he did, and yet his act remains
unparalleled by any similar instance.   Consider that the office
of Georgia Senator was the shining goal of his just aspirations;
that in the judgment of the governor he was the proper recipient of the great trust; that the popular mind coincided with
the governor's views; that the tide in politics was turning
against his party and would sweep him from the Speakership,
and that to lose the Senator's place then might cause its loss to
him forever; consider this situation, and a view of his declina-
tion of the office of Senator will glow upon your admiration as

a sunlit summit of fealty to official trust and party principles whose height will not be often climbed by mortal man.

But he lived to see his course justified. The people of the State kept him in mind. By an unusual popular vote they had this year requested the legislature to make him the State's ambassador in the United States Senate, and their will would have been performed a few days from this sad date when he lies before us wrapped in the slumbers of death. Once by his own act, once by the act of God, the Senatorial crown has been put aside. We are glad he etched into his enduring fame the self-denial which so much exalted his character; we are glad he lived to know that the high trust had been given him by the people of his beloved State; and since he has been deprived by the just will of God of the high position, we will lay the unworn Senatorial robe at the base of his monument and write his great name among those of the patriotic statesmen of our country.

I can not justly omit that eventful period of four years in which, as a young Virginia soldier, he espoused the cause and bravely fought the battles of the Confederate war. When 16 years old, a stripling youth, a boy of handsome form and gallant mien, but spirited as a cavalier, he put on the gray jacket and offered himself for slaughter. It is just such food as war craves, and too often gets. The "flower of the South" decorated the grim battlefields with their slain bodies and made them glorious. CRISP was among the number of that Army of Northern Virginia which Lee, Jackson, and Stuart depended on for victories which made them an immortal fame. The first year brought Manassas, with its unobscured triumph of the Southern army. The second year, the "Seven days around Richmond," when Lee rolled McClellan's outspread columns like a scroll back upon the River James. The third year, Gettysburg, with its first day of glory and its third day of bloody repulse. The fourth year, the Wilderness series of interlapping horrors, centering on the 12th of May, when a whole day's titanic wrestling in garments rolled in blood ended with the fraternal foes confronting each other in rifle range. Through these scenes, with their intermediate events, all equally momentous our young soldier served with his comrades, terminating his field service by his capture in the "bloody angle" of the 12th of May. Imprisonment followed, but when released in 1865, he turned his steps to Georgia and became her loyal, faithful, and honored son. Not once has he claimed political reward for this heroic service in the cause of the South. He knew that patriotism has no price. The tender of life to the state in its peril is only a real tribute of righteous sovereignty, and the offering has no place on any pay roll; it thrusts no key into the public treasury, and makes no demand on the popular ballot. But the record of our comrade is with us his highest honor, and his consciousness of patriotic duty faithfully done is his highest reward.

But the State can not take to itself the keenest pangs which this public bereavement has caused. Let it stand aside in its open sorrow, made expressive by many honoring testimonials, and let it be silent before the poignant grief which wrings the heart of the family whose prop and pride, whose crown and chief, is gone; whose tender fatherhood is now but sweet potential memory. His family life was, after all, his chiefest grace. With a loving nature, he lavished his heart's best gifts on her whom God gave to him and on the children who grew up under his care. If words of consolation could be effectively spoken, we would all speak them in sheer pity for her whose heart is broken by this blow. But no wine press is for the tramping of many feet in concert. She must tread the wine press of her affliction alone. There is One only who can come to her whose comforting is barred by no ceremony and lacking in no quality. "I will not leave you comfortless; I will come to you." And so, if words of counsel were needed by these children, they would be offered by thousands of friendly tongues. But the counsel is not needed. The heritage of a wise father's life is wealth for his offspring. By the memory of his words they will direct their ways. We therefore commit this stricken household to the God who guided their head, and to the memories of his noble life. I do not know how to speak further, in the presence of an audience who knew him so well, of his personal traits and his private life. I am conscious of repeating your sayings when I would describe his genial, hopeful, generous disposition. The smile which lighted his face was an issue of his heart. The face itself inspired confidence; his social mien won affection; his tongue was free from the guilt of detraction; he was kind in speech even when he spoke of his adversaries. Genuine charity had its home in his heart and directed his hand to help the weak and the poor. The masterpiece of Paul's pen, as recorded in the thirteenth chapter of the first letter to the Corinthians, was his most favorite study. His nearest neighbors esteemed and loved him, his friends trusted him, his political opponents respected him.

In early manhood he embraced the faith taught in the Scriptures, united with the church, loved the brethren in its communion, and died in the hope which his religion inspired. Separated now from all that delighted or tried him on earth, he is gone to that mysterious sphere where duty to God will be done in perfection and the joy of the service will be the heavenly rewards.

We may suffer ourselves to be counseled even by death. Meet it we must; meet it daringly we may; meet it reverently we should, for it is designed to be but the priest in the black gown sent to conduct us to the Prince of Life Eternal.

The last object that man beholds on earth is not the state and its officials; not the church and its ministers; not the family of loved ones, and not friends in tears; but the last Being alone with man on earth is Almighty God. In the article of death, after every mortal citadel has been stormed, the eyes of the unassailable soul turns from the delightful scenes as well as from the ghastly horrors of Time to look with clairvoyant power and boundless interest upon the serene eternity of infinite things. In that moment of an indescribable crisis the alone soul looks before it springs, and as it looks it encounters the face of God. The Almighty God! The immortal soul! Face to face! Does the soul reflect the image and likeness of Him into whose face it looks? That is life's crucial question. Blessed in such a crisis are the pure in heart.

In the crucible of every human career, after all fires have burned down and the vessel is cold, there should remain at last

refined and prepared for eternal use an immortal soul which
serenely reflects in character the face of God.

It is well for us who are here, and who know each other's
natures well, to understand that in our inmost unexpressed
thought we believe there is something better than the poor
prizes for which we are all contending.

The question being taken on the resolutions, they were
unanimously agreed to, and in accordance therewith (at 5
o'clock and 55 minutes p. m.) the House adjourned.

PROCEEDINGS IN THE SENATE.

A message from the House of Representatives, by Mr. Chapell, one of its clerks, communicated to the Senate the intelligence of the death of CHARLES F. CRISP, late a member of the House from the State of Georgia, and transmitted the resolutions of the House thereon.

Mr. GORDON. Mr. President, I desire to give notice that on Thursday next, at 3 o'clock p. m., I shall ask the Senate to suspend business to receive resolutions upon the subject to which the message from the House of Representatives relates, and to hear some remarks in connection therewith.

JANUARY 25, 1897.

The Vice-President laid before the Senate the resolutions of the House of Representatives, and they were read.

Mr. GORDON. Mr. President, I submit the resolutions which I send to the desk.

The resolutions were read, as follows:

Resolved, That the business of the Senate be now suspended, that opportunity may be given for tributes to the memory of the Hon. CHARLES F. CRISP, late a Representative from the State of Georgia.

Resolved, That as a further tribute to his memory and in recognition of his distinguished ability as a public servant, the Senate, at the conclusion of these memorial ceremonies, shall stand adjourned.

Resolved, That the Secretary communicate these resolutions to the House of Representatives; and

Resolved, That the Secretary be instructed to communicate a copy of these resolutions to the family of the deceased.

The VICE-PRESIDENT. The resolutions are before the Senate.

ADDRESS OF MR. GORDON.

Mr. Gordon. Mr. President, during the last session of Congress, and near its close, I met on this floor for the last time the great Georgian in whose honor we speak, and whose death an appreciative people so sincerely mourn. Were it permissible to refer to the purpose which brought him from the other end of the Capitol, it would reveal, as his every act, public and private, revealed, the innate nobility of the man.

Charles Frederick Crisp was born in England, but was transferred before his first anniversary to his future home in southwest Georgia. Richly endowed with native abilities and notably with those attributes of character so quickly and infallibly discerned by the open-hearted people of that section, in his early manhood he commanded their respect and enlisted their support. In a district where competition was an impassable barrier against mediocrity, he rose steadily and rapidly in their esteem and confidence until he held without a rival the supreme place in their affections.

Mr. President, if it be true that our temperament and sensibilities and character are permanently affected by the scenes amid which we are reared, this fact would in some measure explain the strikingly attractive characteristics of our deceased friend. His youthful imagination, his gentle nature, receptive and impressible, received their earliest touches and strongest tints from the peculiar civilization, the sunlight, and soft air of that genial clime. His childhood was passed in a locality where an unaffected cordiality was the genius of social life, where daily associations were elevating and refining, and where all nature tended to soften the heart and lift the soul—where home was the synonym of hospitality, and where every open field, made beautiful by the white, the yellow, and the crimson cotton blooms, was rimmed by majestic pines, whose weird music, like the distant murmur of the sea, tranquillized the spirit and turned the thoughts to God.

He was soldier, lawyer, solicitor, judge, national legislator, and Speaker of the House of Representatives. In all these positions of responsibility and trust, in the holier relations of Christian, husband, and father, through all the stages of a great career, in all the activities of life, he was brave, unselfish, strong, and pure. English by birth and blood, he was American in thought, sentiment, and purpose—in every throb of his brain and fiber of his being.

The achievements of his maturer years were but the fulfillment of his early promise. The courage and consecration of the youthful soldier were but the prophecies of the career and crown of the illustrious statesman.

At the age of 16 he won a commission in the Confederate Army under "Stonewall" Jackson. He was with that phenomenal soldier when he fell in the Wilderness. He marched with him, fought under him, felt the power of his majestic presence, and caught inspiration from his dazzling genius and from that inflexible Christian faith and fortitude which are better than genius. Beardless boy as he was, Mr. CRISP met the hardships and dangers of the field with the nerve of a veteran, and endured the privations of prison with the patience of a philosopher.

Mr. President, a character so symmetrical and complete as Mr. CRISP'S deserves to be studied and imitated. Called to an unusual number of positions, he was efficient in all, and in many excelled.   Doubtless this very diversity in his active life, like exercises in training schools for the development of complete physical manhood, was a source of strength in his mental and moral equipment.

As a soldier, he learned obedience to constituted authority, the necessity of promptness, the value and power of organized effort.

As a lawyer, he was taught the efficacy of analysis and of that close, clear, and forceful style of reasoning from premise to conclusion which constitute the strength and charm of his public utterances.

As State's attorney, it was his duty to analyze and denounce crime and to bring the perpetrators to punishment, and he discharged that duty with absolute fidelity and marked ability.

As judge, he was charged with the high function of declaring the law protecting the citizen's rights, his property, his life, and his liberty, and no man ever met these grave obligations more conscientiously and bravely.   The judicial ermine never rested upon worthier shoulders, nor was it ever kept whiter or more immaculate.

As member of the National Congress, he was confronted by the gravest problems of government, and he supported or antagonized measures with an eye single to the welfare of the people.

As Speaker, he had placed in his hands a power greater in many important particulars than that intrusted to the President, and he wielded it, in the judgment of political friend and opponent, with an ability rarely equaled and a courtesy and an impartiality never surpassed.

As professing Christian, he assumed obligations to the Christian Church and to its Divine Founder and Head which he never disowned and never dishonored.

Mr. President, there remains but one other phase of our deceased friend's life of which I wish briefly to speak. In those stations to which I have already alluded his record was far more conspicuous and related itself to a vastly wider constituency. The responsibilities of those public stations, so faithfully met, were to his country, to society, and church. The honors he won by a great career and a noble life are the heritage of the whole American people. But the realm into which I now enter, while far more circumscribed, is infinitely more sacred than any except the church itself. It is due to the occasion, due to my own sense of propriety, to say that the curtain is drawn from the sanctuary of my friend's domestic life by a reverent hand, and that the delicate task is legitimately sanctioned; but it is also due to his memory and to those whom he loved above honors and held dearer than life to say that no home ever lost a nobler head than the home of Mr. CRISP.

Great and lasting as are the honors he won in the public service, sincere and just as are the eulogiums pronounced by his associates in Congress, earnest and universal as are the benedictions of his people, and precious as will be this heritage to the unspeakably bereaved wife and children, yet his constant, daily acts of unselfish devotion as husband and father are to them the richest and most cherished legacy. His unfailing solicitude and tenderness exhibited throughout his busy, absorbing career, and singularly manifested in the very hour of dissolution, when his tongue was no longer capable of utterance, will constitute to this stricken household the sweetest and most hallowed memory.

The life of such a man, Mr. President, is a sermon, a psalm, an inspiration. The death of such a man is a bereavement to society, to the State, to the Republic. Both his life and his death to those of us who served with him and who now survive him are full of encouragement and at the same time of warning—of encouragement to virtuous living in the discharge of duty, and of solemn warning to be ready for the inexorable summons of the mute messenger, who will come we know not how nor when, but will come surely and come to all.

Standing in the gloom of this national loss, the radiance of the highway he trod becomes the more plainly visible. From its opening to its close his career was one of unbroken success. From year to year, from station to station, from one official height to another still higher, his shining course was a constant, continuing ascent, with no blemish to mar, no stain to dim its luster. Holding the great office of Speaker, he declined a seat in this Chamber tendered him by the governor of his State. Though laudably ambitious to represent Georgia in this august body, he turned his back on ambition at the call of duty, whose every command was to him an imperative fiat. He died with the echoes of his last political victory still ringing in his ears. He died near the convening of the legislature which, in obedience to the formally expressed and emphatic popular will, would have sent him triumphantly to the Senate as a partial recompense for his previous self-abnegation.

Providence denied him the coveted seat in this Chamber, but called him, as we confidently hope and believe, to an infinitely more exalted station in the invisible, everlasting convocation of the just.

ADDRESS OF MR. GALLINGER.

MR. GALLINGER. Mr. President, in response to the request
of the distinguished senior Senator from Georgia, whose
eloquent and touching words of eulogy have charmed our
ears to-day, I will very briefly pay tribute to the great Georgian, whose virtues and accomplishments are matters of
history. It was my privilege to serve with CHARLES FRED-
ERICK CRISP during the Forty-ninth and Fiftieth Congresses, and it is an exceedingly pleasant memory that we
were friends as well as associates during those four eventful
years. Mr. CRISP had not then risen to the high eminence
as an orator and parliamentarian that he achieved in later
years, but even then, almost at the threshold of his Congressional career, he impressed himself upon the House as
a man of marvelous gifts and commanding powers. I recall
more than one instance when he surprised his associates
by an exhibition of tact, ability, and skill in the management of legislation, while his occasional outbursts of fervid
oratory are not forgotten by his fellow-members. At times
Mr. CRISP was intensely partisan, as all strong men are, but
he was always courteous and usually fair. The rancor of
debate left no scars on his tender mind, and the turbulent
waters of party strife did not soil the purity of his soul.
Looking back over the years that have come and gone to
the time that I passed with Mr. CRISP at the close of the
Fiftieth Congress, my heart goes out to him even as it did
when we daily met. His kindly words are remembered,
and his strong and pervading personality is vividly and
tenderly recalled. But the good friend, the courtly gentleman, the intellectual giant is no more. At the very zenith

of his fame—the chosen leader of his party associates and the idol of his State—he was summoned from earth to the great beyond. Mr. CRISP has gone to his reward, to receive the plaudit of "Well done, good and faithful servant."

Mr. President, it is a single blossom that I bring to be laid on the casket of my dead friend; but the tribute, though brief, is sincere and heartfelt. A man of marvelous powers, grand achievement, and noble purposes has passed away. The place he so well filled in the halls of legislation is vacant; but his place in the hearts of his family, his friends, and his countrymen will forever be bright and glorious. Farewell, thou man of strength and grandeur; of tenderness and heroism; of mighty achievement and exalted purpose. Earth's work is done, life's fitful fever is ended, and the joys of a better world are the reward for the faithful performance of earth's duties and obligations. Farewell the true friend, the convincing orator, the great Speaker, a fond and tender farewell.

ADDRESS OF MR. GORMAN.

Mr. GORMAN. Mr. President, my purpose on the present sad occasion is briefly to express my great personal esteem and my high admiration for a great leader in the public councils of our country, whose life added luster to American character and illustrated the possibilities in American political life.

It can not be too often noted and emphasized that there is no insurmountable bar to preeminence in the politics of our country when to personal traits of exalted character there are added incorruptible integrity, firm resolution, and positive courage. When these high qualities are graced with kindliness of disposition, urbanity in intercourse, and a high sense of justice and fair dealing toward adversaries, we have that truly American character which was illustrated in the public life of the late CHARLES FREDERICK CRISP.

His early schooling was obtained in the camp, upon the march, and in the very forefront of the battle. It was amid the hardships, restraints, and sacrifices incident to four years of civil conflict that he laid fast and sure the foundation of self-reliance, indomitable resolution, and high purpose, which in a few years brought him forward as one qualified to lead and to shape the course of political affairs. His promotion was rapid. Admitted to the bar in 1866, he was raised to the bench in 1877, and from that high position was elected to the House of Representatives in 1882. There, in committees, on the floor in debate, and in earnest work, he so impressed his political associates that in the Fifty-second Congress his party elected him Speaker of the House— the most exalted position within the gift of the House, and second only to the Presidency in point of power in our system of government.

These accomplished results illustrate not only the high character and attainments of Mr. CRISP, but they emphasize the possibilities of popular government, whose highest honors are at all times open to the free competition of those who are worthy to fill them.

The public life of Mr. CRISP illustrates the truth of the remark that "nothing is denied to well-directed labor, and nothing is obtained without it." Leadership in the House exacts the most constant and assiduous labor from those who aspire to its high emprize, and can not be purchased at a lesser price. His administration of the duties of the Speakership, during periods of intense excitement and amid the conflicts of contending interests, left not a sting among his party adversaries, nor failed to bring intensest satisfaction to his supporters. He was preeminently fair, considerate, just, and impartial, and left the well-earned reputation of a great Speaker. A like career on this floor was frustrated by the rude hand of death immediately after the people of Georgia had expressed their purpose to elect him to the Senate.

There must have been in such a career a dominating principle to which thought and action were at all times subordinated. We shall not improve occasions like this if we fail to eliminate the motive and the principle which made the public career of Mr. CRISP so worthy of study and so full of noble example. He was a partisan in the purest sense of that word. He had satisfied his conscience that more substantial good, more positive progress was possible to the country from the principles, measures, and organization of the political party to which he was attached than was possible from any other organization. Hence his advocacy, as well as his opposition, was directed at all times to the triumph before the people of the principles and measures of his party. But that partisanship was destitute of every unworthy motive, free from all asperity, and unattended with epithet, innuendo, or aspersion. Those who differed from him listened to his earnest advocacy, confident that it was inspired by sincerity and prompted by a high sense of duty. If to "party he gave up what was meant for mankind," it was because he identified his party with all that was best and safest for the general welfare of the people, the progress of the country, and the advancement of her civilization.

By disposition, as well as from conviction, he was a conservative of that form of government and that distribution of its functions which under the Federal Constitution can alone render permanent the blessings of popular government. At the same time he was a pronounced radical in his conviction that all power emanates from the people, and that the administration of government can never be safe and successful unless it be conformable to the wishes and opinions of the people as expressed by their representatives, and that the regular, orderly, and authentic expression of public opinion was obligatory at all times upon the legislative and the executive departments of the Government.

Such exalted principles qualify and modify partisanship into patriotism, and teach the lesson that intensity of advocacy is at all times compatible with a just consideration for the convictions of an adversary. That was the preeminent characteristic of the political career of Mr. CRISP. In the most excited and embittered contests over measures like those for the repeal of the election laws or the different phases of the tariff discussion, he exhibited the highest qualities of leadership, but at the same time the fullest recognition of the same earnestness of conviction in his opponents.

Without the brilliancy of oratory or the graces of rhetoric, his very earnestness and the manifest sincerity of his character became persuasive and convincing, and made him a natural leader and his party willing and enthusiastic followers. There was in his personality every element which made association pleasant and agreeable. With warmhearted geniality he won the affections, while his dignity of bearing impressed all who came within its influence. But there was no compromise of principle within his nature; what conscience approved, expediency could not compromise. It was that full and complete subordination of expediency to principle that carried into the Speakership the integrity of the judge and clothed the politician with the ermine of justice.

It was natural that such a character should impress the people far beyond the borders of Georgia; hence his popularity was as widespread as his party, and in every State he won the respect and confidence alike of Democrats and Republicans. Citizens of every party recognized the purity and sincerity of that "hope" for "our beloved country" when uttered by him upon being elected Speaker.

No review of his public and private character would do justice to our departed friend which did not emphasize that unselfish devotion to duty which declined the appointment to the Senate by the governor of Georgia because he was more useful to his party at that time in the House. The seat in the Senate was the goal of all his hopes, the crown of his ambition. But the opportunity of his life came at a moment when duty to his party demanded its declension. He was equal to the sacrifice, and set aside his personal promotion for the good of his party. There is a deep sadness in the fact that after such unselfish devotion to duty death should have robbed him of his reward when tendered by the suffrages of the people of that great State of which he was a noble citizen and an honored Representative.

My acquaintance with him was close and intimate; my confidence in his judgment, discretion, and ability was full and complete. He measured up to every occasion, and never was a flaw or crevice found in that armor of principle, integrity, and zeal for "our beloved country," which enveloped him like a "garment of praise."

ADDRESS OF MR. BERRY.

Mr. BERRY. Mr. President, I met CHARLES FREDERICK CRISP for the first time when I came here in 1885. He was then serving his second term in Congress, and had already attracted attention as a man of ability and high character. Subsequently I knew him intimately and knew him well. We lived together in the same hotel in this city for eight years. During the sessions of Congress I saw him daily. I saw him in his associations with his family, with members of Congress, and with numerous friends from all sections of the country. That he was a man of high character and splendid ability I need not say. That he met bravely and was equal to each responsibility and that he did his duty faithfully and well to his constituents and his country is known to all.

Mr. CRISP was one of the few men in public life of whom it could be truly said that he was always equal and never superior to any place or station where duty called him to go. He rose steadily and continuously in the public estimation and grew greater year by year as his duties and responsibilities increased, and he was more honored and loved at the time of his death than at any time before. The most prominent and striking traits in his character as they appeared to me were his self-poise and remarkable self-control, his uniform cheerfulness, his great patience and kindliness toward all with whom he came in contact, his quick perception, and great power to condense and convince in argument. I saw him every day and many times each day during the exciting and heated contest for Speaker in December, 1891. I saw him at the time when many of his friends thought he was beaten. I saw him in the hour of his victory, and no one could detect in his manner or bearing the least sign of despondency in the one instance or elation in the other. I saw him after the contest was over, when the pressure came upon him for committee assignments. From early in the morning for many days until late at night his rooms overflowed with members of the House of Representatives, Senators, and many others. He saw and heard all who came, and never for one moment did he lose his patience, his cheerfulness, or his kindliness of manner. If he felt the criticisms and abuse which came from the disappointed—and he did feel it, for he told me so long afterwards—he made no sign and uttered no complaint, and I think now that it was these high and admirable qualities in his character that enabled him afterwards to lead and control his party so absolutely in the House of Representatives. Many strong men, many great men, have presided over the House of Representatives; but I think none of them ever surpassed Mr. CRISP in his ability to lead, and none ever had more devoted and willing followers. That he was a great Speaker and possessed qualities that peculiarly fitted him for the position all will admit, but that which made him really great was his devotion to duty and love of country.

These were the same qualities in his character that caused him when a lad of 16 years of age to march forth to battle for his home, his people, and the faith of his fathers, and this same devotion to duty and love of country remained with him in the exalted position he afterwards obtained. And he was as true and loyal to our common country and to the flag of the Republic when presiding over the House of Representatives as he had been true and loyal to the flag of the South when he upheld it and faced death upon the battlefields of Manassas and Spottsylvania.

The greatest lesson taught by the life of Mr. CRISP is that it shows the possibilities of success for the American youth. It is the glory of our Republic that the poorest boy in the land, if he has the courage to be honest and upright and the energy to persevere, may aspire to any place within the gift of the American people.

Mr. CRISP returned from the war in 1865, a youth of 20, absolutely without means or influential friends; without the advantage of college training; dependent alone upon his own resources; and yet at the age of 45 he had served as district attorney, judge of the superior court, member of Congress, and Speaker of the House of Representatives, and had discharged the duties of all these positions in such way as to command the respect of friend and foe. During all of his career he never forgot the people of Georgia; those with whom he had marched and suffered in time of war; those who had been loyal and true to him in every ambition of his life. He never believed that he was wiser than they; he never sought to secure what is called a national reputation by antagonizing or sacrificing the people of his State. He was true to them, and they supported him with a devotion and unanimity seldom if ever surpassed.

The last contest he ever made, the last speeches he ever delivered, were in a contest within his own party upon a great question of party policy, and in this, as in the past, he was in full sympathy with and true to the great body of his constituents who had so often honored him, and they showed their appreciation by giving him an overwhelming majority for a seat upon the floor of the Senate of the United States.

The last conversation I ever had with him was upon his return from that canvass, where he had met the then Secretary of the Interior in joint debate. He told me that his physician had insisted that he should quit the canvass and of his regret for the necessity. He spoke of his failing health, the intense pain that he suffered, and that he feared it was the beginning of the end. He did not speak of it lightly, nor did he speak of it in any gloomy or despondent way, but calmly and courageously, as a brave man would speak of something that could not be avoided and that he was ready to meet without fear, but that he hoped might be postponed for the sake of those dependent upon him.

I never saw anyone more devoted to his family than Mr. CRISP. During all the years that we lived in the same house no one ever heard him speak an unkind or impatient word to wife or child. He was the intimate friend of and loved by all children; he was deferential to all womanhood and courteous to all manhood. He was always a gentleman in his manner and deportment; a Southern man in his instincts and feelings; a Southern soldier true to that cause until its flag was furled forever. He never paraded his services, nor did he ever express regret or offer excuse for the course he had pursued. When he laid down his arms and pledged his word for future allegiance to this Government, he kept his promise in letter and spirit, and when he arose to the high position that he afterwards reached, he was as true and loyal to the Government of the United States as the men whom he had faced in battle. The people of the South have much cause to love and honor his memory, and the people of the entire nation have much cause to be proud of such a citizen.

ADDRESS OF MR. MILLS.

Mr. MILLS. Mr. President, there are some reasons which
have impressed me that I should join the people of Georgia
and the friends of her distinguished son in paying to his
memory all the honors which the living can pay to the dead.
The remains of his father and mother have for many years
been sleeping in the warm and generous bosom of Texas.
Side by side with her own children, Texas has seen that
their graves are kept green.   There are still living in Texas
those who knew intimately the father and mother and who
cherish their memories, and who knew the son in his young
manhood, whose name in after years became a household
word around all their firesides.   If there were no other
considerations which moved me, this would constrain me
to go with the people of Georgia and drop a flower for
Texas in the grave of Georgia's distinguished son.   But
there are other considerations which to my mind make it
appropriate for me to speak of him.   During the great civil
war—the greatest in the annals of mankind—he and I were
soldiers on the same side.   We fought with those who lost.
He served with the army which defended Virginia; I with
the army which defended Georgia.   We both passed through
all the vicissitudes incident to the life of a soldier.   One
by one the old gray-jackets are passing away.   Even those
who, like him, entered the service at 16 come fewer and
fewer to the annual reunions.   During the last summer I
went to a reunion of Confederate soldiers in a county in
Texas from which I had a company in my regiment num-
bering more than a hundred.   Not many returned from
the bloody fields of Tennessee and Georgia, and of those

who did return there was not one present to call the roll. As a comrade in arms, I would come to his bier and help his loved ones lower him to that last sleep from which only the reveille of Heaven shall awake him.

In that fearful contest it was my fortune to be three times severely wounded, two of them on the same day. I was sent from the field to the hospital at Lagrange, Ga., where I received from the mothers, wives, and daughters of Georgia soldiers the kindest care and the tenderest nursing, without which I should be sleeping to-day in the Confederate cemetery at Lagrange. I remember how like angels they hovered about our rude cots, and while pouring balm into our wounds, they poured consolation into our ears and hope into our hearts. I remember how noiselessly they passed from cot to cot, watching the life struggle of the torn and lacerated soldiers, ever ready with hand and heart to help the sinking pulse to strike back toward life, and the lusterless eye to relume and burn again with life's brilliancy. Lingering long after the sun had gone, folding tenderly the winding sheet around those appointed to die, and administering the opiate prescribed by the surgeon to soothe the suffering to sleep, they bade all good night with lips and eyes burdened with prayers, and hied them to their homes. At early dawn their footsteps were heard again at our bedsides, to go over and over again the labors which their brave and patriotic hearts had made a labor of love. These are memories which are indelibly stamped upon my brain. How could I ever forget the people of Georgia!

I come now in this hour of grief, when the hand of the Reaper has cut down a son whom she honored and loved, and one who loved and honored her, and take my place with her in rendering to his memory every tribute which pride and affection can pay to the memory of her loved and lost son. In life he served her faithfully and well; he achieved honors for himself and heaped honors upon a noble people whose servant he was. I remember when he came a Representative to the Forty-eighth Congress. He had been a lawyer of prominence at the bar of his State. From that he rose to the bench. He was equipped with the knowledge and accomplishments that such positions give to a man of labor. He soon stood among the leading members of the House, and easily maintained the place which thorough study and preparation had enabled him to win.

The House of Representatives is as much unlike the Senate as the stormy waters of the Atlantic are unlike the waveless waters of the Dead Sea. The House is the focus of the concentrated power and passion of the people. There the popular heart beats with its strongest pulsation. There the popular voice speaks with its clearest emphasis. It is a field where the people assemble in the galleries and look on and are quick to express approbation or disapprobation. They applaud, laugh, shout, and jeer the combatants. They are severe, merciless critics. The leader who puts on the armor of Saul but can not wear it like Saul will soon discover his mistake. In the House the party leader must be ready for battle at any moment, for he knows not at what moment his forces may be assailed. He stands in the arena of combat, and to command the confidence of his followers he must be able to give and take the blows of battle in such a way as to retain the approval and affection of his comrades. This is the ordeal through which all leaders of the House have passed and must continue to pass. In this ordeal CHARLES FRED-

ERICK CRISP bore himself well, and continually won his way toward the top. In the Fiftieth Congress John G. Carlisle, of Kentucky, was elected Speaker. His seat as a member of the House was contested. He very properly declined to appoint the Committee on Elections, because he could not with propriety appoint the judges who were to pass upon his own title. The Democratic caucus designated several gentlemen who were authorized to select that committee and appoint its chairman. I had the honor of being the chairman of the committee appointed by the caucus. When we met, I proposed the name of Mr. CRISP as chairman of the Committee on Elections, and he was unanimously chosen. He discharged the duties of that exacting and laborious position with conspicuous ability.

He was a good lawyer, a good student, well informed in the rules of parliamentary law, and an able debater. He was conciliatory and kind in his disposition, and grappled his friends to him with hooks of steel. In the Fifty-second Congress he was elected Speaker of the House, and so discharged the duties of that high station that he was reelected as long as his party was in power. So strong was his hold upon the affections of the people of Georgia that they had designated him as a member of this body, and had he lived until the 4th of March next he would have taken his seat here ; but on the 23d day of October, 1896, "God's finger touched him, and he slept." There is now nothing left us but to bow with resignation to the decree which sooner or later will come to us all. Peace to his ashes!

ADDRESS OF MR. CARTER.

Mr. CARTER. Mr. President, on my appearance in the Chamber this morning the eminent senior Senator from Georgia [Mr. Gordon] kindly accorded me the privilege of addressing the Senate briefly on the character and services of CHARLES FREDERICK CRISP.

When I first became acquainted with Mr. CRISP he was in the prime of life. We stood together before the Speaker's desk and took the oath of office at the same time as members of the Fifty-first Congress. My service was then beginning. He had to his credit six years of honorable and distinguished service in that body. He was an accomplished parliamentarian and a veritable legislative gladiator. He was a modest, unassuming man.

In the stormy scenes of that memorable Congress he was a constant and forcible but not a noisy participant. Without boisterous demonstration as a representative of his party views, he resisted the parliamentary reforms proposed by the opposition with a skill which commanded the respect of his opponents and the affectionate admiration of his party associates.

I can recall him now as a calm, self-reliant debater, rising in the midst of the excited Representatives to present and support his convictions concerning the moving cause of the existing commotion. His self-control became contagious, and agitated members quickly became attentive listeners. His career in that Congress gave notice to the country that in any parliamentary emergency liable to arise in the history of the Government Mr. CRISP would prove one of the most competent and thoroughly reliable of American statesmen.

The Speakership of the next House of Representatives was accorded him by his party associates in recognition of the eminent ability displayed by him in the course of his service in the House. While his partisanship goes unquestioned, we observed with intensified regard the moral courage which impelled him to adopt views he had previously opposed when those views became confirmed and approved in the severe test of parliamentary experience.

It was as a new member of the House of Representatives that my first impressions of this great man were formed. He was a generous man; he was a just man; he was all that is embodied in the phrase so often applied to him—a fair-minded man. To the new member of the House he extended the hand of cordial good-fellowship and welcome. His great experience and logical mind always stood at the ready disposal of the new member. It is the recollection of his many acts of considerate kindness to which I ascribe the affectionate regard in which his memory is held. While others in studied phrase analyze his character and the lessons of his life, I gratefully avail myself of the sad privilege of recognizing his early and unfailing courtesy to me by placing the tribute of my humble praise upon his honored grave.

ADDRESS OF MR. DANIEL.

Mr. DANIEL. Mr. President, a noble character has disappeared from the conspicuous scenes of American public life—a man who had the good will and the confidence of all who knew him, and the affection of all who knew him well.

The death of CHARLES FREDERICK CRISP is a great national loss. To the people of his own State it is a poignant affliction, and to the many friends whom he made in his career in the capital city of the United States it is a source of deep personal grief. A number of those who knew him and associated with him in the House of Representatives and in the conferences and consultations of our public affairs have analyzed the peculiar features of his mind and have painted those virtues which the public had thoroughly realized that he possessed. I shall not attempt, Mr. President, to do more for my part than to allude to a few of the conspicuous characteristics of Mr. CRISP and to express my own profound sympathy with those upon whom his death has so heavily fallen.

I think it may be said of him that no man has taken so conspicuous a position in public life, has exercised such great responsibility, has been thrown in conflict with such great antagonisms and such influential interests, who at the same time has so conducted himself as to achieve more thoroughly the good will of all who came in contact with him.

Mr. CRISP was a man of solid and substantial character and of useful gifts. That character was always thrown as a great weight upon the side which he deemed to be right, and those gifts were always employed in patriotic interests.

It may be truly said of Mr. CRISP that he was a patriot. There was nothing small, nothing mean, nothing narrow, nothing sectional, in any offensive sense, in the characteristics or in the history of the man. He was a manly man, a man of broad, humane, and catholic sympathies, of high and noble purposes, and he never thought of, much less did he ever condescend to, questionable methods or offensive methods in achieving his purposes.

I think that the great weight which Mr. CRISP acquired in the House of Representatives was due to the equilibrium of his temperament and to the well-ordered adjustment of his fine faculties. His mental and moral virtues were well fused; they made a compact and wholesome unit. Everyone always knew where he stood; everyone felt the good influence of his presence, of his association, and of his counsel.

I had much in common with Mr. CRISP in the courses of our varied lives. We entered the army of the Confederate States in the same command, in that immortal band known as "the Stonewall Brigade," which made its debut in history on the first field of Manassas, and bore its shredded battle flags in the last conflict at Appomattox. He entered that brigade when a boy of 16, as a member of the Tenth Virginia Infantry. He acquired the reputation among his comrades of being a good soldier. He never seemed to desire the honors or shows of military distinction, but he became an officer before he was yet a man. He was content, as were the great body of patriots all over this land who gave themselves to a cause and to a flag, to do his duty as he thought it should be done, and was content that it had been done.

Mr. CRISP was a man who had in him the elements of inevitable success. He was steady of purpose. When he set his head in any direction, he persevered and continued to persevere in that direction. Concentration is the secret of success. Mr. CRISP possessed concentration. He did not seek many things at once. He took in hand the thing that was before him; he did it well, and he was always called up higher because he had done well that which went before.

It has been well said, Mr. President, by a fine writer, that self-control is the highest form of self-assertion. Mr. CRISP possessed self-control. He was well-poised; he was always self-possessed. Whatever of ability and of talent he possessed were always ready and available. His judgment was almost always a wise judgment. He was a man well fitted to elevate and honor the bench. He was judicial in bearing, judicious in decision. He was a good man. His heart was in the right place. His instincts made him do right without reflection in those moments of exigency which give little time for reflection. His studious disposition made him find the right when it was involved in perplexities and complications.

The House of Representatives, Mr. President, is a forum which puts to sternest tests the qualities of men in public life. Of all the theaters in which political ambition and political usefulness are exercised it is the most exacting. In the House of Representatives, among the many brilliant men who represent the different sections of this great and diversified country, there is soon an evolution to the front of the strong men. We often see there men of great scholastic ability making little impression upon the affairs of the country. We see men of brilliant oratorical qualifications and forensic talents making little headway in influence, and reaching but small consummations. It is because there is necessary to success in that body a peculiar combination of talents, a mixture of tact, judgment, courage, skill, ability to speak, and ability to keep silent—a certain practical common sense withal, a certain indefinable and predominant quality which we can never exactly estimate, which we can never thoroughly analyze, which we can never paint and fully describe, but which is ere long discovered to be in one man or another when large assemblies are brought together. We all know that Mr. CRISP was well versed in parliamentary law, able in debate, oftentimes powerful and effective in oratory. We all know that he was fair-minded, discreet, and capable in counsel. But, however we attempt to analyze his qualities and qualifications, we all realize that he had such as made men honor and follow him.

I had the pleasure of first making the acquaintance of Mr. CRISP in the Forty-ninth Congress. He was then a young member, gathering his earlier experiences of Congressional life. He never seemed to seek position of conspicuous distinction. He never made a speech for the mere sake of making it. He never showed any desire for display or effect or applause in the speeches which he did make ; but when he did speak, he spoke at the proper time, he said the right thing, and in effect his services had already at that early stage in his career marked him as a man who would lead and influence and guide men, and would make his mark in the affairs with which he was associated in conducting. Year by year he became more prominent. He came in collision with the ablest minds in American politics. It is enough to say that he always held his own. He was thrown in most fierce antagonism with the great interests which influence legislation and in hot conflict upon the most partisan questions which have ever engaged the minds of the American people. He came to the front rank of the disputants. In his addresses he always commanded attention. In his positions he always attracted support. In his decisions as Speaker and on the policies he pursued he made but few mistakes. In his conduct of party affairs he always showed that tact and wisdom which achieve results, or come as near achieving results as it is possible. Though, sir, he was in the heat of battle for many years, although he was thrown in antagonism with the ablest minds, although he was often suddenly precipitated into debate with the keenest and subtlest intellects, although day after day he had to show preference between one man and another or make sharp and far-reaching decisions, the fact speaks that at the end of that career all who were associated with him, whether in sympathy or conflict, whether in concurrence or disagreement — all say, "This was an honorable champion; this was a just man; this was a true patriot; this was a noble and useful character; this was a good citizen."

All bowed their heads as the cortege which bore his remains passed by, and all would fain throw a flower upon his tomb.

I knew Mr. CRISP in other capacities than that of legislator. I had the privilege of enjoying his personal friendship, of meeting him often in genial and social scenes. This but attracted me the more to him.

Mr. CRISP was a man of fine manners and address, natural and unaffected. He had the instinctive courtesy which is not that of mannerism, but which is born in the heart and which expresses itself in the many small and nameless kindnesses which make life worth living. He was a genial and kind companion; he was a true friend; and though, sir, there are many who have decorated his name with more fitting praise than my poor words convey, there are none here who mourn him more deeply or who will more sincerely cherish his memory.

Georgia has sent to both Houses of Congress many able and brilliant men. Among them the name and fame of Mr. CRISP will always shine with a calm and steady luster.

ADDRESS OF MR. BACON.

Mr. BACON. Mr. President, the many touching, beautiful, and appropriate eulogies which have been paid to the memory of our friend both in the House and in the Senate leave little need that I should attempt to add anything, however brief. I may be pardoned, however, for a few words before asking for the adoption of the resolutions submitted by my colleague.

It is a great thing for one to be an acknowledged leader among men. It is still greater for one to be recognized by voluntary acclaim as the leader among a concourse of those who are themselves leaders. But greater than this high distinction is the honor, when such a one falls on that high arena in the thick of the combat, that the strife ceases and that there are offered by Representatives and Senators of all parties and sections—as well those who have contended with him as opponents as those who have striven with him as allies—such tributes to his character and achievements as in the anticipation would fill the measure of any man's ambition.

Most tenderly will these words of affection and praise be cherished by those of his own blood, by the host of men knit to him by the ties of friendship, and by the State which has most lovingly and proudly enrolled his name upon the list of her most distinguished sons.

Mr. President, I need not say more of those qualities and achievements which have won for him the praise and admiration not only of his associates, but also of the nation; and yet I can not forbear to say that as I have listened in the House and Senate to the words which have been uttered during the consideration of these resolutions the thought has come to me that if it were mine to write his epitaph in the portrayal of his personal character, I would inscribe but the single line, "All men loved him."

Twice, Mr. President, within less than three years has the State of Georgia stood a mourner within this Chamber lamenting the loss of a cherished son who held her commission in the National Congress. The first of these had been for nearly twelve years an honored member of this body. He to whom we to-day do honor, while never a Senator, occupied a peculiar relation to the Senate. As has been told, he was once appointed a Senator, but duty, whose voice to him was a command, denied him entrance here; again, two years later, at the time when he was stricken down as with a lightning shaft, his foot was on the very threshold of this Chamber. Already chosen by the well-nigh unanimous voice of the people expressed through a primary election, with no opposition to his election by the legislature which was to assemble within a week, the arm of the State was already outstretched to place within his hand her commission to him as one of her ambassadors to this high council of the representatives of States.

From one point of view there was never a sadder picture of disappointed hope. The dream, the ambition of his life, was to be a Senator of the United States. Neither in public nor in private had he disguised its avowal. From boyhood he had set his gaze upon it, and through all his manhood it was the goal of his desire. All undaunted by obstacles, he strove to reach it. Step by step for thirty years, unwearied, never failing in resolve, always steadfast in endeavor, he had climbed the steep ascent, he had scaled the rugged cliffs, he had gained the dizzy height where shone the prize, when in a moment the sun of his life went out at noonday!

The vainness of regret stifles not the tender emotion which this contemplation must inspire in every sympathetic heart. When the full span of life has been accomplished, when the life work to which one has set his hand has in his labor found full fruition, still the death of even such a one, the end of a career where no more remains for achievement, nevertheless brings inevitable sorrow to all who have the instinct of life and who shrink back from the mystery of death.   But deeper must be the emotion, more tragic in its nature the catastrophe, when in mid career one falls in life, as fell in estate the great cardinal, while he—

Bears his blushing honors thick upon him.

Mr. President, it is sad to see even the shrunken and withered giant trunk sway in the blast and fall before the fury of the storm ; but when in the peaceful sunshine, when no winds blow, when no cloud is in the sky, all suddenly falls the green and sturdy oak, we start back shocked and dismayed.

Humanity can not suppress its moan in the presence of death.   Around it there is such impenetrable mystery ; between the living and the dead there is such an unspeakable, fathomless, unmeasured gulf.   Beside the bier there is only remembrance of the great change, the life that has gone from among us and can never return.   In the presence of the physical ruin the heart echoes the wail of Antony by the dead body of Cæsar:

Are all thy conquests, glories, triumphs, spoils,
Shrunk to this little measure ?

And yet, sir, sad as is this contemplation, wrung and torn as are the hearts of those who mourn his loss, who can view the life of our departed friend, so rounded and so symmetrical, so steady in its upward progress, so full and overflowing in its fruition, and not say—it may be through blinding tears, but still in loving pride—'tis well?

And, sir, while I would not dry one tear that is shed for him, while I would not suppress one moan that breathes out the sorrow of those who mourn for him, yet I take heart in the glad thought that in those things which made our friend beloved of all, in those things which made him a leader among men, in those things which marked him in the nation's view as a great man, in all these things he is not dead and can not die.

More lasting than the marble which will mark his last resting place, in the unfading memory of all who knew him in life, in the imperishable archives of his State and of this great nation, will ever live the enduring record of this good and great man.

And not as a memory only will he live. The teaching of Revelation finds its strongest confirmation in the conviction of the inner consciousness that the sun of this life does not go down into an eternal night. Who is there of the most skeptical who believes that the soul and the intellect which looked out from the eyes of CHARLES FREDERICK CRISP, and beamed in his countenance and inspired his lips, have perished with the body that we have tenderly laid away from our sight? There is that within that tells us it can not be. When or how we know not, but the undying yearnings for the loved ones gone before tell us that we shall meet again.

In the drama of Ion, the young heathen Greek, forewarned by the Oracles of impending death by violence, comes to part with the maiden he loves. She asks him, "Shall we meet again?" He replies that he has asked that dread question of the hills that look eternal; of the streams that flow on forever; of the stars amid whose azure fields his spirit had walked in glory. To that question they all had been dumb. "But now," he adds, "while thus I gaze upon thy living face, I feel the love that kindles through its beauty can never wholly perish. We shall meet again."

Mr. President, I ask for the adoption of the pending resolutions.

The resolutions were unanimously agreed to; and (at 4 o'clock and 20 minutes p. m.) the Senate adjourned until to-morrow (Tuesday), January 26, 1897, at 12 o'clock meridian.